LIFEBLOOD

Tom Becker

LIFEBLOOD

DARKSIDE
BOOK 2

Orchard Books
New York

An Imprint of Scholastic Inc.

Text copyright © 2007 by CPI Publishing Solutions.
Cover illustrations © 2007 by Studiospooky.
First published in the UK by Scholastic Ltd in 2007.

ISBN-13: 978-0-545-03742-6
ISBN-10: 0-545-03742-5

Library of Congress Cataloging-in-Publication Data
Becker, Tom.
Lifeblood / by Tom Becker — 1st ed.
p.   cm. — (Darkside ; bk. 2)
Summary: As Jonathan searches London's Darkside for the same murderer
that his mother was seeking when she disappeared twelve years earlier, it
becomes clear that it is Jonathan who is being hunted.
ISBN 978-0-545-03742-6
[1. Supernatural — Fiction.   2. London (England) — Fiction.
3. England — Ficton.   4. Horror Stories.]   I. Title.
PZ7.B3817177Li 2008
[Fic] — dc22

200751180

10 9 8 7 6 5 4 3 2 1   08 09 10 11 12

Printed in the U.S.A.

Reinforced Binding for Library Use

First edition, September 2008

Book design by Phil Falco

For Youngy, for battles won

Prologue

The envelope had arrived for him seven days ago. He had returned to his desk late one evening to find it sitting there waiting for him, a large black rectangle elegantly tied up in red ribbons. No name had been written on it, nor was there any indication that it had traveled through the mail. Looking back, he supposed that he should have been more cautious about opening it, but he had assumed it was one of his colleagues playing a prank on him. Policemen were like that sometimes.

So Sergeant Ian Shaw wasn't worried when he untied the ribbons and carefully slit open the envelope. Curious, yes, but not worried. It was only after he'd seen what was inside — flicked through the photos, read the sculpted, handwritten note telling him precisely what he had to do, and precisely who was going to see the photos if he didn't — that his hands began to shake, and he slumped down in his seat and put his head in his hands.

Seven days ago: He had barely slept since. Shaw had so much to lose. Ever since he had been drafted in to investigate the kidnappings of two boys, the policeman's life had been turned upside down. He had been able to reunite one boy with his mother, and the second — well, although technically Jonathan Starling remained missing, Shaw knew where he was, and that he was happy and safe. The solving of the case had taken place in a blaze of publicity, and Shaw had been at the very center of it. A promotion and several high-profile newspaper interviews had quickly followed. His colleagues looked at him with a new-found respect (and no little jealousy), while his wife spoke of him with a pride that he had never before heard in her voice.

So instead of alerting his family and his superiors to what was happening, or telling the blackmailers to get lost, one night Sergeant Shaw crept down to the station base-ment and began rooting through old case files. It didn't take him long: The Starling case was very recent, after all. After that, things were relatively simple. He put one phone call through to the lab, ordered one test, and received one batch of results. The technician had sounded surprised to be ordered to run the test, but he did it anyway. Ian Shaw was a name that carried some weight around the force these days.

Now he was in Rotherhithe, standing on the Thames Path and looking out over the south side of the river. The envelope had given him precise instructions of where he was to wait. Staring out over the choppy waters, Shaw thought glumly to himself that this location was the perfect setting for shady deeds. Even in the bright sunshine tourists rarely ventured this far east, preferring the wide, bustling walkways near Blackfriars and Waterloo. At nearly ten o'clock on a biting December night, this part of town was deserted.

He had traveled to the waterfront on foot, as instructed, past the cavernous old wharf houses that had once welcomed home the trading vessels of the British Empire, which crisscrossed the oceans in search of a profit. Now the wharf houses had been converted into plush apartment blocks, and decorated with window boxes, satellite dishes, and burglar alarms. Even so, Shaw felt he could almost hear the echoing cries of long-dead sailors and dockhands.

The waves down below him began to lap more insistently against the waterfront. He checked his watch again. Given the preciseness of the instructions, he had a feeling that whoever was coming to meet him would be prompt. Not for the first time, the thought occurred to Shaw that he had placed himself in danger by coming here. The note had told him to come unarmed, but it was an unnecessary instruction. He had never fired a gun in his life, and didn't intend to start now.

The current was picking up, foam bubbling on the crests of the waves. Shaw saw a movement in the darkness over the Thames, and suddenly realized why he had been told to wait here.

A low barge was cutting through the waves toward him with a speed and a sleekness that Shaw could not have believed possible from such a craft. It was steam-powered, yet the engine hummed rather than roared, and the steam rose out of the funnel in soft rings. The barge was painted entirely black, and had it not been heading directly for him Shaw doubted whether he would have seen it at all.

The boat pulled up dangerously close to the side of the waterfront, somehow maintaining its position on the rolling waves. There was a movement from the back of the barge, and a hand beckoned to Shaw to jump aboard. The policeman took a look around and, seeing that no one was watching, swung his legs over the bars and planted his feet on the edge of the walkway.

Even though the barge was keeping remarkably still, it was far enough from land to make the jump a difficult one. Shaw hesitated, only for the hand to move again and a voice from somewhere shout, "Come on, man, hurry up!" Reacting instinctively, the policeman sprang off the side of the waterfront, landing with a heavy thump on the wet prow of the barge. Immediately, a hand reached down and dragged him up, and as the barge moved away from the waterfront, Shaw was marched briskly into the cabin. His unseen guide closed the door behind him, preferring to stay out on deck.

Two men were waiting for the policeman in the cramped quarters of the cabin. The first was a huge walrus of a man who rose to greet Shaw with a beaming smile, as if he were meeting an old friend. On a plate in front of him, a pile of chicken legs had been devoured, leaving only the bones and a few scraps of skin. The walrus's tall companion could scarcely have looked more different. In his pressed suit and top hat, he seemed to be heading for a ballroom dance rather than a clandestine meeting. His features were twisted into a perpetual curl of disdain that helped jam a monocle in his left eye. When he raised his hat in a greeting, Shaw was surprised to see that his silver hair rose up into the air in stiff peaks, like dried paintbrushes in a pot.

"Sergeant Shaw!" the second man said in a nasal voice. "I recognize you from the photographs. I'm glad you could make our rendezvous."

"I suppose you're not going to tell me your name," Shaw replied icily.

A look of scorn crossed the man's face. "Why should I care whether you know my name or not? It's Nicholas de Quincy, not that it will do you any good. You won't find *me* in your files."

Sergeant Shaw's heart sank. Ever since he had received the envelope he had hoped against hope that his blackmailers were ordinary, run-of-the-mill hoodlums and thugs. During the Starling case he had taken glimpses into a different, darker world that he hoped never to experience again. In vain, it seemed.

"Humphrey Granville," said the first man helpfully. "Pleasure to meet you, sir."

He wiped a greasy hand on his shirt and proffered a

handshake. Still dazed by the turn of events, Shaw accepted it. De Quincy watched with a look of undisguised contempt. He turned to Humphrey.

"Is that idiot Rafferty sober enough to be left in charge of the barge?"

Humphrey shrugged. "Probably not. But he's been driving these boats since he was able to stand up. I think he'll be all right."

"Excuse me . . ." Shaw tried. "But what is going on here?"

"A typical policeman — cutting straight to the point!" scoffed de Quincy. "That will make things so much easier. I presume that you received the envelope I left you exactly one week ago?"

"I did, and I have to tell you now that those photographs . . ."

De Quincy held up an elongated hand. "I don't care," he said starkly. "Given the fact that you are here, I am guessing that you followed my instructions? Because we both know what will happen to you if you haven't. . . ."

"You even think about sending those photographs, and I'll . . ."

"Anger . . . excuses . . . blustering threats," said de Quincy. "I have heard it all a million times before. *Did you follow my instructions?*"

Shaw nodded again.

"And what did you discover?"

The policeman reached into his pockets and drew out a piece of paper. "Well, I went through the Starling case files and found the fluorescent orange hair — the one taken from the female bounty hunter Starling identified as Marianne. I sent it to the lab with the piece of hair you gave me, and told one of the technicians to run a DNA test on them both."

Both Granville and de Quincy leaned closer.

"And?" Granville said, with breathless excitement.

Shaw consulted the piece of paper. "Obviously, the boys in the lab can never be definite about this sort of thing, but having analyzed the DNA, they're ninety-nine percent sure that these people are closely related."

Granville whooped and punched his fist into his palm with glee.

A thin smirk spread across de Quincy's lips. "Well, well, well. That is decidedly interesting news."

"Thank you so much for your help, Sergeant," Granville enthused. "We are most grateful."

"It's been an absolute pleasure," Shaw said sarcastically. "Now give me the photographs!"

De Quincy sighed delicately. "I'm afraid I can't quite do that just yet."

"You promised!"

"I promised not to show them if you did what I told you to. And I won't. You have been *very* helpful. And if I need some help in this part of London again, I know who to call on."

With a shout of rage, Shaw made for de Quincy, arms outstretched, only to see Granville raise an old flintlock pistol and point it straight at him.

"Regretfully," the small man began, "I have to ask you to step away from my colleague. If you do move any closer, I will be forced to shoot you. I know you are accustomed to slightly different weapons, but let me warn you that this gun fires real bullets and I am a fine shot."

Breathing heavily, Shaw backed away from de Quincy, who sneered at him.

"You're just as pathetically predictable as the rest of

them. Now get out of here! Rest assured I will be in contact with you again."

Granville gestured at the door and ushered Shaw out of the cabin and back into the icy night air.

"Edwin!" he cried out to the pilot, still hidden away at the stern of the barge. "Drop the sergeant off, and then take us home."

The barge changed course instantly, cutting back toward one side of the river. Confused and disoriented, Shaw couldn't even tell whether it was the north or the south bank. As the barge purred up to a small wooden jetty, Granville gestured with his gun again.

"I'm sure you can make it home from here," he said, still cheery. "Farewell!"

Shaw alighted back onto dry land, frustration welling in his eyes at the brutal unfairness of his situation. From the dark prow of the barge, the two men watched him turn on his heel and head back into London.

"Ninety-nine percent certain!" Humphrey Granville chortled.

"Yes," mused Nicholas de Quincy. "Marianne's a Ripper, all right. Time to start the bidding."

1

The torrent of blood came gushing down without warning, hitting Jonathan Starling before he could react. The last thing he had seen was the playing card with the malevolent face of the Jack of Knives grinning up at him from the table, and then a thick red waterfall engulfed him. The force of the blast sent him sprawling from his seat, and into a dazed heap on the floor.

As he looked up, coughing and spluttering, his eyes stinging, a face peered at him over the table. It was the dealer, a huge beast with fierce eyes and off-white tusks protruding from his mouth. He was wearing a black suit with a bloodstained butcher's apron fastened over the top of it. With a shrug, he calmly gathered up the rest of Jonathan's hand of cards.

"The boy is out of the game," he announced. "Do we have a new player to fill the seat?"

There was a clamor from the small crowd behind Jonathan, and two well-dressed gentlemen leapt over his body to claim the vacant chair. Just as the taller of the two appeared to have won the race, the smaller man punched him viciously in the kidneys. As his competitor crumpled and groaned, the smaller man pushed him aside, chuckled with glee, and sat down at the table. The tusked dealer sighed and began to hand out another round of cards.

Jonathan gingerly picked himself up and moved away from the roped-off game. His hair was coated with blood, there was a roaring sound in his ears, and his shoes gave out an apologetic squelch every time he took a step. He rubbed his face with his sleeve in a forlorn attempt to clean himself up, a move that only served to smear more red across his cheek.

With hindsight, perhaps playing Gorey had not been his best idea.

Late at night in the Casino Sanguino, and the main hall was quiet; it would be another couple of hours before the serious gamblers took their places. Heavy purple drapes had been drawn across the window, and cards were drawn and bets laid under the flicker of gaslight. The air was thick with hushed desperation. Sweaty, disheveled men rolled dice with a manic gleam in their eyes, certain that this time they would be lucky. Hulking brutes with rolled-up sleeves stalked the room, keeping a beady eye out for any gamblers making money. Winning a game was one thing, making it out alive another matter entirely.

Jonathan fished inside his pockets and checked his pocket watch. The man he was expecting should have arrived by now. Threading his way between tables, Jonathan scanned the hall. To his right, a game of blackjack threatened to degenerate into a brawl as the dealer began clubbing one of the players over the head. On the far side of the room, a frantic group braced themselves as the dealer spun again on the Wheel of Misfortune — perhaps for the last time. From time to time a howl of pain flew over from the roulette table, where the balls had a nasty habit of flying off the wheel and into the eyes of unwary gamblers. In these surroundings, being drenched in blood actually helped Jonathan blend into the background. No one gave him a second glance. If he had tried to walk around like this anywhere else in London, he would have been locked up. Then again, he was in Darkside. Things were different here.

As he passed a raucous game of hazard, Jonathan caught sight of the man he was looking for. A smartly dressed man with a gleaming silver cane, he moved with disdain through the hall: Lorcan Bracket, one of Darkside's finest confidence tricksters. The con man was strutting toward the center of the room, where a spiral staircase rose like a metal finger over a hundred feet up into the air. At first glance, it appeared that the tall structure was unfinished and led nowhere, but in fact it was the only way to reach the most fabled and dangerous game in the Casino Sanguino: plummet.

Craning his neck until he could see high up into the vaulted ceiling of the hall, Jonathan could just make out a suspended platform moving through the air like a magic carpet. A series of steel cables connected it to a motor that powered along a track cut into the ceiling, propelling the platform onward. Jonathan knew that a group of gamblers was sitting up there, playing a game where the stakes couldn't possibly be higher. The rules to plummet were fiendishly complex, but there was one simple factor that tended to occupy the minds of those who played it: If you could knock all your opponents off the platform, then the pot was yours. Cheating and cheap shots were actively encouraged, and the action more often resembled a high-altitude riot than a game.

Bracket began to ascend the staircase, a spring in his step. Jonathan took a deep breath and slipped quietly after him. As they climbed, the gamblers beneath them became smaller and smaller, while the sound of their screams and shouts dimmed. Jonathan hurried to catch up with the con man. There was no point in hiding now. As Jonathan drew closer, he heard Bracket humming a jaunty tune to himself. Unlike Jonathan, he didn't know that one of the plummet players that evening was waiting for him. Lorcan Bracket was walking straight into a trap.

As the two of them emerged at the top of the staircase, Bracket glanced at Jonathan, and raised a lofty eyebrow at his bloodstained appearance.

"This is a game for men, you know. I'd run along if I were you."

"I'll take my chances," Jonathan replied.

"If you get in my way, you'll be the first going over the edge. Don't expect any sympathy from me."

As Bracket spoke the platform came into view, steam pumping from the motor as it clattered along the track in the ceiling. It slowed as it moved past the staircase, giving Bracket and Jonathan the chance to jump aboard. The cables gave a slight shudder as they absorbed the extra weight of the two new players.

Judging by the coins stacked up on the playing cloth, this game of plummet was well under way. Through a haze of cigar smoke, Jonathan could make out a shabby figure at the far end of the table, absentmindedly scratching his cheek with a long nail as he perused his cards. A battered stovepipe hat was rammed far down over his head, bearing the scars of years of maltreatment. His stubbled, craggy face was deep in thought. The other three players had pulled their chairs around to the other side of the table, and were watching the shabby figure fearfully. After a long pause, the dealer cleared his throat delicately.

"Your move," he said.

Elias Carnegie, private detective, wereman, and Jonathan's ally, yawned. "This is a crucial part of the game, Jak, and I don't like being rushed. Unless you want to end up like Wilson did half an hour ago, I'd give me a little more time. They're still scraping him off the floor."

The wereman grinned menacingly as he caught sight of the new player sitting down stiffly at the table.

"Well, well, well! Lorcan Bracket! I had a feeling I might see you tonight."

The con man inclined his neck by way of acknowledgment. "It's no secret that this game is a favorite of mine."

"Even so . . ." Carnegie leaned forward confidentially. "It's a stroke of luck, because I need to talk to you about something."

"Really?"

"You see, you took something recently that wasn't yours, and the owner asked me to get it back. And now here you are, all alone, with nowhere to hide! I'd call it a coincidence, but I don't believe in them."

A sneer broke out on Bracket's face. "Neither do I, wolf-man. I heard you were looking for me. I thought it might be best to deal with you up here."

He nodded at the other three players, whose nervous expressions suddenly vanished. They rose as one, drawing bludgeons from their belts. Bracket pressed a button on his cane, and a sharp blade came shooting out from the tip. Anticipating trouble, the dealer dropped his cards and dived underneath the table. Jonathan gasped. It seemed they hadn't been the only ones setting a trap.

As the men advanced on Carnegie, the detective bowed his head. A low growling sound rumbled from the back of his throat. Jonathan took a fearful step back: He knew what was about to happen. Now everyone on the platform was in deep trouble, including him. Carnegie's entire body began to shake violently, his fists clenched so tightly his knuckles whitened. Even underneath the crumpled suit, it was possible to make out his muscles rippling and expanding. When he finally looked up, his face was covered in gray hair, his teeth were pointed and canine, and his eyes burned with rage. He was no longer a man, but a beast.

Bracket's men paused momentarily before mounting a screaming charge. Carnegie bellowed in response, and hurled his chair at the men, hitting one of them dead in the chest and knocking him off his feet. Jonathan felt the platform wobble, and clutched a cable for support. Looking down, he could see the denizens of the Casino Sanguino continuing their infernal dealings, unaware of the drama taking place far above their heads.

If Bracket's plan had been to encircle Carnegie, he hadn't counted on the speed of the detective when in his wolf form.

As the men closed in, the beast threw a shuddering body block at one of the henchmen, sending both of them rolling away from the rest of the players. Using the momentum of their tumbling bodies, Carnegie kicked out with his legs and sent the henchman up into the air and off the edge of the platform. Seeing his companion so summarily dispatched, the other man paused. It was a fatal error. The beast was up and on him in a flash, teeth bared, his claws slicing through the air. The henchman ducked and weaved, but there was nothing he could do in the face of such an onslaught: A thumping cuff from a paw sent him, screaming, toward the casino floor.

Bracket swore and backed away from Carnegie, keeping his sword-stick trained on him. As the wereman advanced, Jonathan noticed that the henchman who had been hit by the chair had managed to get back to his feet. Creeping around Carnegie's blind side, the man raised his bludgeon high above his head and prepared to strike. Almost without thinking, Jonathan lowered his head and charged. The collision took the henchman by complete surprise, knocking the wind out of him and sending him staggering toward the platform edge. There was a look of shock in his eyes as his foot fell on thin air, and then he was gone.

A few seconds later there was an almighty crash from the casino floor, and a howl of pain.

Carnegie whirled around at the commotion, and stared down at Jonathan. For a second there was no recognition in the beast's eyes, only blank hatred, then he spun back toward Bracket. The con man aimed a nervous swipe with his sword-stick, which the wereman coolly knocked aside. He seized Bracket by the waistcoat, lifted him up, and held him out over the edge of the platform.

"Please . . . don't let me fall!" the man stuttered.

"You know what I want. Give me the ring."

Bracket blanched. Carnegie sighed, and held him farther out over the hall. "You're a heavy man. Can't hold you forever."

"Wait!" His hands scrabbling desperately through his pockets, Bracket pulled out a small diamond ring and tossed it in Jonathan's direction.

"That the one, boy?"

"Looks like it."

"Good."

The private detective gave Bracket a final wolfish grin, and then let go of his waistcoat. With a scream the man hurtled toward the ground, legs and arms flailing like a drowning swimmer before crash-landing onto the roulette table. The danger over, the beast in Carnegie began to recede. He dusted off his hands and turned back to Jonathan.

"Thanks for the helping hand there, boy." He cast an appraising eye over Jonathan's blood-soaked appearance. "Been having fun?"

"Loads. Can we go now, please?"

The platform had completed a circuit of the hall's ceiling, and was trundling back toward the spiral staircase. A relieved Jonathan hopped back onto the top step and relative safety. He turned to see the wereman grinning.

"Hang on a minute."

Carnegie stooped down and lifted up the tablecloth, revealing the quivering form of the dealer.

"Looks like there's only one player left, Jak. Where's my winnings?"

2

Edwin Rafferty trudged up the steps leading out of the Midnight, shielding his eyes from the glare of the sunlight on the Grand. The wan Darkside morning was brilliant compared to the interior of the Midnight, where patrons downed mysterious drinks in complete darkness. Edwin had lost track of how much time he had spent there; it might have been hours, it might have been days. It was a surprise to discover that he was still unscathed, his meager valuables untouched. Many visitors to the Midnight discovered to their cost that a pitch-black bar was the perfect hunting ground for pickpockets and cutthroats.

As his eyes slowly came to terms with the light, Edwin took in the filthy majesty of Darkside's main street. In his younger days, he had courted violence by standing out on the sidewalk while dashing off sketches of the surrounding buildings, and he was familiar with every smashed window and rusty railing. Generally the Grand was quiet in the mornings, catching its breath in between the eruptions of violence that marked the night. The crowds that converged in darkness had thinned to a smattering of passersby and the occasional clip-clopping of a horse-drawn cab. High up over the street, smoke drifted listlessly from tall chimneys.

This wasn't to say the Grand was necessarily safe. The air was still heavy with sullen menace. Darksiders flung suspicious glances and threatening glares at one another and kept their hands free at all times, in case they had to defend themselves. Men huddled together in doorways, sharing grudges and plots in urgent whispers. Across the street, a couple of urchins scuffled in the gutter.

Edwin ran a calloused fingertip over the scarred remains of his left ear — a familiar, comforting action. Deep down he knew that he shouldn't have been drinking, and he felt the familiar aftertaste of guilt in his mouth. He had hurried to the Midnight as soon as he had navigated the barge back from Lightside. In truth, he should have returned to his house and started work on another painting, but as Edwin found himself descending the familiar steps, he reassured himself that it had been a stressful journey. It was only natural that he would want to unwind afterward. One drink wouldn't hurt.

The truth — something that Edwin could now admit to himself — was that he was scared out of his wits. He had always been the weakest of his friends: *Brother Spine*, they called him, with heavy irony. And now he had been dragged into a dangerous plot that pitted him against the deadliest people in Darkside. In an ideal world Edwin would have told the others to go away and would have had nothing to do with their scheme, but in this world he was flat broke and the potential rewards were almost beyond comprehension. If everything worked out he wouldn't have to worry about money ever again. He could move to a better house, buy himself a fine new wardrobe, regain the trust and respect of his family. For years they had treated him with scorn and contempt. They could never understand why he was happier in an artist's studio than on the deck of a ship, or why he felt more comfortable with a pencil in his hand than the tiller of a boat. But if he was rich again, they would have to accept him. Maybe he could even buy the Midnight.

With these attempts to comfort himself revolving around his head, Edwin turned down the brim of his hat and prepared himself for the long stagger home. Ramming his hands deep into his pockets, he felt his fingers brush against a piece of paper. He pulled it out and unfolded it. His bleary eyes struggled to decipher the handwriting, but eventually Edwin was able to make out the note. It read simply:

You will be my answer.

The hairs on the back of Edwin's neck began to tingle and his mouth ran dry. He read the note a second time, and then a third. It still stubbornly said the same thing. Edwin glanced up and down the street, trying to see if anyone was watching. There were suspicious characters at every turn, but none who appeared to be taking a special interest in him.

He stuffed the note back in his pocket and began walking cautiously down the Grand, his mind in a daze. Edwin certainly hadn't written the note and he couldn't remember seeing it before. Someone must have slipped it into his pocket in the Midnight. But why would anyone want to do that? Unless . . .

His brain offered him one distinctly unpleasant answer. Edwin picked up his pace, walking in quick, shuffling steps. As if to acknowledge the new threat, a sharp, cold wind picked up, while the sun dipped behind a gray cloud.

There was a sudden shout from behind Edwin. He whirled around, only to see a newspaper boy trying to hawk a copy of *The Darkside Informer.*

"'Ere, you want one, mister? It's my last one."

"No!" Edwin cried, his eyes wild. "Stay away from me!"

The boy shrugged. "Suit yourself. *Weirdo,*" he added under his breath.

Feeling exposed, Edwin turned off the Grand and headed down a narrow street called Rotten Row. He had walked this route a thousand times, knew every loose paving stone and curve in the wall, knew it was the fastest way back to his home. He could walk it after a week in the Midnight and never miss a step. If anyone did try to follow him, he would lose them in the dense warren of backstreets.

Despite these comforting thoughts, Edwin was still ill at ease. A shout from across the street sent him scurrying into an alleyway that ran between two rows of houses, where he broke into a shambling run. His tattered shoes splashed through dirty puddles, and his knuckles scraped against the walls as he went. If he was being chased, his pursuers were running in silence — the only noise Edwin could hear was the ragged gasps of his own breath. Dimly he thought that he should look over his shoulder and check, but he was too frightened.

Edwin stumbled on, dodging wash lines and dogs, heading deeper into the mazelike heart of Darkside. The alleys became narrower and narrower, until the houses loomed so closely together that they blocked out what little sunlight there was. His lungs screamed in protest and he could feel a stitch developing in his side. He was already beginning to tire. Even as a young man, Edwin had never been an athlete, and he was in dreadful shape these days. Only the adrenaline racing through his system was keeping him on his feet.

He was nearly there, though, he noted with satisfaction. His home was now only three streets away. There he would be safe. Edwin risked a glance over his shoulder, and saw nothing except a back gate flapping open and shut in the breeze. Unable to run any farther, he staggered to a standstill, nearly falling to the ground with exhaustion. He bent double, desperately searching for his breath. After wheezing for a few minutes, Edwin hauled himself upright and continued walking.

He was in perhaps the dingiest alleyway in Darkside. The surrounding houses all appeared to be empty; their windows smashed and doors hanging off their hinges. Streaks of blood ran down the walls, and there was a smell of rotten meat in the air. Probably a dead dog or a rat, Edwin thought glumly. The pain in his side was excruciating.

It was at that moment that a silhouette moved out from one of the derelict houses and blocked the path. In the half-light, it was difficult to make out who the figure was. Then it spoke, and it suddenly became horribly easy.

"Brother Spine?"

Edwin gasped.

"Brother Fleet! I-it has been . . . too long, my friend."

"Dear Brother Spine," the voice continued mockingly. "Still so weak. So predictable. Did you not even *think* of going another way home?"

"It's the quickest way. . . . I'm very tired. . . ."

"Of course it is. Try not to worry. You'll be able to rest very soon."

Edwin began to back away from the silhouette, his arms outstretched in a pleading gesture.

"B-brother," he stammered. "Surely you wouldn't hurt *me*. It wasn't my idea. I tried to stop them, but they wouldn't listen to me. . . ."

"I'm sure you did," the figure replied soothingly. "No one ever listened to poor Brother Spine, did they? And now no one ever will again."

Whimpering, Edwin stumbled backward over a garbage can, and landed hard on the wet cobblestones. He looked up and for the first time realized the true horror of his fate. The air was ripped asunder by a deafening, inhuman shriek, followed by a high-pitched scream. And then there was only silence.

3

It was early morning, and the office of Elias Carnegie was flooded with pale light. Carnegie was ensconced in the chair behind his desk, peering suspiciously at the recovered diamond ring.

"Funny what people get attached to," he said. "I wouldn't swap a leg of lamb for this."

Jonathan settled down onto the threadbare couch by the window. "I don't think it'd fit you, anyway," he replied lazily.

The wereman glared at him. "Why don't you go and clean up? All that blood on you is making me hungry, and I'd hate to have to eat you."

Sighing, Jonathan got up and went next door to the bathroom. As he relaxed in the murky stillness of the bathwater, his mind drifted over the events of the past couple of months. Only eight weeks had passed since the Darkside bounty hunter Marianne had tried to kidnap him in the middle of London. It felt like a lifetime. His world had been turned upside down with the discovery that there was a secret borough of London filled with evil creatures, where his mom, Theresa, had been born. She had been missing for twelve years, and Jonathan didn't know whether she was dead or alive. But being here — in Darkside — made him feel somehow closer to her; that a part of his soul was being fed after years of starvation.

He had pressed Carnegie endlessly for more information about his mom's disappearance, but the wereman proved unusually evasive on the subject. It was enough to drive Jonathan crazy with frustration. He felt that Carnegie knew more about Theresa than he was letting on, but no matter how hard he pushed, he came up against a blank wall. In many ways, it reminded him of growing up with his dad.

Thinking of Alain Starling sent a pang of guilt through Jonathan. His dad was still recuperating in London, following another one of his "darkenings," fits that left him mentally and physically shattered. If it hadn't been for Alain, Jonathan would have died at the hands of the vampire Vendetta. Both father and son had been lucky to escape with their lives. Jonathan hoped that, under the watchful eye of family friend Mrs. Elwood, Alain was getting better, but the guilty truth was that he hadn't been back to see for himself. It was as if Jonathan was unwilling to leave Darkside in case, like his dad, something happened that meant he was unable to ever return.

After the high of the Casino Sanguino, a more melancholy mood had descended upon Jonathan. He hauled himself out of the bath and rubbed himself dry with a towel. By the time he had pulled on pants and a shirt and wandered back into the office, Carnegie had company.

". . . I came here as soon as I got your message. Have you really retrieved my ring?"

The speaker was Miss Felicity Haverwell, a well-to-do middle-aged woman who had been taken in by a typically complex confidence trick organized by Lorcan Bracket. She wrung her hands together with anxiety as she spoke.

Carnegie nodded. "Yes, ma'am. Though not without a struggle. . . ."

Miss Haverwell's eyes widened. "Did you have to hurt him to get it back?"

"Let's just say he won't be running around for a while."

"Where's the ring? Can I see it?"

Carnegie grinned. "Of course you can. As soon as you pay me."

Her face fell, and she began rummaging through her purse. "Oh, of course . . . I didn't mean to . . ."

Jonathan glared at the wereman, who cut in hastily. "It's not that I don't trust you, Miss Haverwell. It's just that I've had some problems with clients in the past, and I find it's best to work by set rules. Your ring is fine, see?"

He held out a long hand covered in scraggy black hair. The ring lay sparkling in the center of his palm. Miss Haverwell's eyes lit up at the sight of it. She reached out cautiously and slipped it on her finger, sighing with relief.

"Oh, thank you, Mr. Carnegie. I never thought I'd see it again. It means so much to me, you understand . . ."

"Yes, I'm sure," he replied, bored.

"It's the key to my whole fortune . . ."

"Obviously."

"Without it, how could I do this?"

She pressed down on the diamond, sending a spray of mist out from the heart of the jewel. The air was immediately filled with thousands of tiny iridescent bubbles. Jonathan gazed at them in wonder, feeling them brush lightly against his skin as they drifted down toward the ground. He was just thinking that the ring was the most amazing toy he had seen, before the room went suddenly and violently black.

He was dimly aware of a hand shaking him by the shirt.

"Come on, mister. Get up," a voice pleaded through the fog.

Jonathan was in the middle of a deep, mysterious dream involving his family, and he seemed so close to understanding everything that he really didn't want to wake up, but the voice wouldn't go away. Reluctantly, Jonathan came to, groaning.

He was lying where he had fallen, in the corner of Carnegie's office. The wereman was slumped facedown on his desk, emitting soft, guttural snores. While they had been unconscious someone had ransacked the office, overturning furniture, pulling out drawers, and scattering pieces of paper all over the floor. A small boy was leaning over Jonathan, wide-eyed with concern.

"You all right?" he asked.

"Not sure yet. Who are you?"

"Jimmy Dancer. Arthur Blake at *The Darkside Informer* sent me here to give a message to an Elias Carnegie." He looked dubiously at the snoring detective. "Is that 'im?"

Jonathan nodded, the movement making his head throb. Groggily, he got to his feet and went over to the desk.

"I've tried everything to wake him up," said Jimmy. "Even screamed down his earhole."

"Glad you didn't try that with me. Hang on a sec."

Rubbing his face vigorously, Jonathan tried to collect his thoughts. He knew that there was only one thing that would stir Carnegie from his stupor.

"Look for a dirty brown bottle on the floor. It'll be somewhere among the mess."

After a couple of minutes of scrabbling around on his hands and knees, Jonathan located the bottle underneath a broken chair. On the fading, peeling label, someone had scrawled CARNEGIE'S SPECIAL RECIPE. He didn't know exactly what the ingredients of the recipe were, and he didn't want to. He did know that the concoction functioned as a potent high explosive, and he had a horrible feeling that Carnegie occasionally drank it.

Gesturing at Jimmy to stand well back, and firmly clamping his nostrils shut, Jonathan uncorked the bottle and wafted it under Carnegie's nose. With a roar the wereman shot bolt upright, his claws protruding. Jimmy screamed with fright.

"It's all right, Carnegie! It's me!" Jonathan shouted.

The wereman blinked with surprise. "What . . . what happened?"

"That woman — Miss Haverwell. Her ring must have contained some sort of sleeping spray. It knocked us both out. She's gone through all your stuff. Probably taken anything valuable."

Carnegie muttered a foul oath, and rose stiffly to his feet. "What did I say? First rule, boy. Never give them what they want until they pay you. I don't care if they're five years old, or ninety-five. Come on, then. Time to find the good lady and have a quiet word with her."

He turned to leave, then paused, noticing Jimmy for the first time. "And who are you?"

"I've got a message from Mr. Blake at *The Informer*," he squeaked, carefully passing Carnegie a folded scrap of paper. The detective read the note, glanced at Jonathan, and then read it again.

"I guess Miss Haverwell's going to have to wait," he said finally.

The Informer was Darkside's only newspaper, and was almost as old as the borough itself. Given the prevailing attitude toward people asking questions and prying into the business of others, it was amazing it had kept going for so long. Its survival was partly due to its audience's insatiable desire to read about audacious crimes and villainous schemes. The newspaper also provided a more practical function: In a world without television, the best way to sell something was to advertise in its brown, crackly pages.

Though the newspaper was tolerated, it was by no means popular. In Darkside, journalism was a perilous way of making a living. The offices of *The Informer* were based far away from the center of the borough, tucked away among the great tanning factories in the east. Jimmy led Carnegie and Jonathan there on foot, never managing more than a few yards in a straight line before turning off down another shortcut. Behind Jimmy, his head still fuzzy, Jonathan kept his eyes peeled for trouble. He might have become a little more familiar with the Grand and Fitzwilliam Street, but there were still large swaths of Darkside that remained a mystery to him. And anyway, he knew that no street here was truly safe.

The smell of burnt leather announced that they had entered the tanning quarter, a stench so strong that it threatened to overwhelm Jonathan's nostrils. Imposing, black-bricked factories swamped the surrounding streets with poisonous clouds of smoke. On the wall of the nearest building, someone had daubed a ten-foot-high pair of bull horns in red paint. Jonathan shuddered. Even by Darkside's standards, this was a grim part of town.

"Are we nearly there yet?" he called out.

Jimmy pointed out an anonymous, dilapidated building sandwiched between two factories. There was no sign over the front door, no clue to what took place inside.

"That's it there."

Carnegie strode purposefully through the front door and into a deserted office. Inside it was dark and cool, although the smell from the neighboring factories seeped through the cracks in the windowpanes, tainting the air. The floor shook with the clatter and rumble of machinery in the room below. Jonathan shot Jimmy a questioning look.

"Printing presses," he explained. "They run through the day so we can get the paper out during the night. Mr. Blake'll be upstairs."

As they headed up a rickety flight of steps, Jonathan tugged Carnegie's sleeve. "Working for a newspaper around here doesn't look like much fun."

"It's not. To be a journalist in Darkside, you've got to be pretty strong, or pretty desperate."

"What's Mr. Blake like?"

"He's a little bit of both."

The windows in the upstairs offices of *The Informer* had been boarded over, and in the candlelight Jonathan could make out a handful of people hunched over their work. They spoke to one another in terse, wary sentences. No one looked pleased to see the new arrivals at the top of the stairs. Jimmy led them over to a battered writing desk, where a reporter was poring over some proofs.

Jonathan blinked. Arthur Blake was a small barrel of a man. Rolls of fat sprouted up above his collar and poked out from the end of his sleeves. At any minute, it seemed as if his shirt buttons would lose the battle to cover his enormous belly, and shoot off through the air like bullets. A permanent sheen of sweat glistened on his forehead, and he breathed in loud gusts through his nose. Looking closer, Jonathan was struck by his dark brown eyes, which hinted that a keen intelligence bubbled beneath his physical ungainliness.

Arthur addressed Carnegie without looking up. "You took your time."

"We had some problems back at the office. Anyway, we're here now. You left me a note. What's going on?"

"There's been a murder. Nasty one, too. Come up to the editor's office and I'll tell you all about it."

Arthur hauled himself up from his chair and waddled over to the far corner of the office, where a small staircase led up to a private room. As they climbed up the steps, he called out to Carnegie over his shoulder, "Who's the boy?"

Carnegie sighed. "His name's Jonathan. Jonathan Starling."

The reporter stopped in his tracks. Then he shuffled

around and shot Carnegie a meaningful glance. "Starling as in Theresa's son?"

The wereman nodded slowly.

"What is it?" asked Jonathan. "How do you know my mom?"

Arthur Blake paused for a second, before answering somberly. "Everyone here knows Theresa Starling. This is where she used to work."

4

Jonathan gripped the banister tightly, suddenly fearful that he might fall. His head was spinning. His mom had worked here — spent hours, days, weeks of her life here. How many times had she walked up and down this very staircase? As Jonathan struggled to take in the information, another, darker thought occurred to him.

He turned and faced Carnegie. "You knew this," he said. "All this time, and you never told me."

The wereman sniffed loudly, and looked away. "Time wasn't right," he said eventually.

"It's never right, though, is it?" Jonathan shouted. "You're just like Dad — hiding things from me. Why won't you tell me about my mom?"

Anger pounded his heart like a hammer on an anvil. Jonathan drew himself up to his full height and stared balefully at the wereman, who smiled a cold, sharklike grin in response.

"Have you got a problem with me, boy?" he growled softly. "If so, I'd advise you get over it *very* quickly."

For a few seconds neither of them flinched. Muscles stayed taut, eyes didn't blink. Then, with a small sound of disgust, Jonathan broke away and continued up the staircase. Behind him, Arthur raised an inquisitive eyebrow at Carnegie. The wereman shook his head, and said nothing.

When he reached the top of the stairs, Jonathan saw that a man was seated behind the desk in the editor's office. With his head in his hands, and a look of intense concentration on his face, the man looked as if he carried the weight of the world on his shoulders. His face was lean and sallow, and there was a haggard look in his eyes that hinted at late nights and snatched hours of sleep. A stubbly beard roamed over his chin, while his wiry black hair had been cropped closely to his skull. The creases and crumples in his clothing suggested that the man hadn't changed them for the better part of a week.

"Gentlemen," said Arthur, "this is Lucien Fox, editor of *The Darkside Informer*. Lucien, this is Carnegie and Jonathan Starling."

Lucien looked up at the mention of Jonathan's last name, and subjected him to a keen inspection. Then he glanced at Arthur, who nodded.

"Come in," the editor said, in a surprisingly strong baritone. "It's a pleasure to meet you. Your mother was a fine reporter, Jonathan."

As he came out from behind his desk to greet them, Jonathan saw that Lucien's left foot was splayed slightly inward, restricting his movement to a shuffling limp. He shook their hands and smiled.

"Now, what tales has our star reporter been telling you?"

Arthur winced, dabbing at his damp forehead with a handkerchief. "I wish you wouldn't call me that," he said wearily.

"It's true, though, isn't it?" For the first time, a wry smile appeared on Lucien's face. "And exposing the truth is what *The Informer*'s all about."

"So you keep telling me," Arthur replied. "I thought it was about trying not to get killed."

The editor hobbled over and clapped the large man on the back. He turned to Jonathan.

"Arthur loves to pretend he's modest and nothing special, but don't believe a word of it. He's got a keener sense for a scoop than all the other journalists in Darkside put together. He's uncovered hundreds of the foulest deeds in this borough. Remember the plague epidemic at the MacPherson Cotton Factory? Workers were dropping like flies, but no one could figure out what was causing it. That was until our star reporter turned up and deduced that a disgruntled employee was poisoning the water supply. And that's only *one* of his more famous stories! I could go on . . ."

"I'll be amazed if you don't," Arthur replied sourly, although Jonathan suspected that the reporter was secretly quite enjoying the eulogy.

Carnegie grinned slyly. "Most of the people around here prefer their crimes to remain uncovered. You must be a popular man. How many people have tried to kill you?"

"Enough," Arthur replied gloomily. "They'll probably get me one of these days."

"Really, it's something of a miracle he's still alive," said Lucien. "Good thing, too. Without Arthur, *The Informer* would be sunk." He limped back behind his desk and sank into his chair with relief. "Well, now that we're all acquainted, why don't you tell Mr. Carnegie why you called him over here?"

Arthur went over to the window and peered outside before carefully closing the blinds. Satisfied that no one could see them talking, he settled himself down in a stiff-backed chair, which groaned under the weight.

"To be honest, I stumbled across this by accident." He glanced up. "I was down at Devil's Wharf, questioning one of the dockers about some decidedly fishy nighttime deliveries that were taking place around the Rafferty warehouses. As we were talking, word started flying around that a body had been found in the Lower Fleet. Seeing as I wasn't getting any useful information, I thought I'd take a chance on the scoop and see what I could find. Now I almost wish that I hadn't."

There was a haunting, lyrical quality to Arthur's voice. Jonathan found himself leaning in closer to listen to him. The clatter of the printing presses below them faded into a background hum.

"I was on the verge of giving up and going home when I came across a tiny alleyway in the middle of the Lower

Fleet. Its contents were . . . not a pretty sight." He paused. "A man's body was lying in the middle of the alleyway. Or what was left of it — he looked like he'd been ripped apart by a pack of wild animals. The sight of it was nearly enough to make me sick.

"At that time there was no one else around. The alleyway looked derelict — there was no guarantee that anyone would come to claim the body or take it away. So once I'd caught my breath, I made a search and tried to find out who the poor soul was."

The thought of rifling through the pockets of a dismembered corpse sent a shudder of revulsion down Jonathan's spine. By contrast, Carnegie's ears pricked up, and the bored expression on his face vanished. "What did you find?"

"The usual stuff: loose change, matches, a bunch of keys. Nothing that could help us identify him."

Lucien leaned forward. "Which is where you come in, Carnegie. We want you to help us find out who this man was, and what happened to him."

The wereman tapped his fingers together thoughtfully. "Well, this is all very interesting, but before we talk business I need you to answer a question for me. People get murdered in Darkside all the time. You write up what happened, people buy your newspaper, life goes on. *So stop messing around and tell me why you're taking so much trouble over this one!*"

Suddenly his voice was as cold and hard as steel. Lucien and Arthur glanced at each other, and eventually the former nodded.

"Look," said Arthur, "I've spent the last few years of my life documenting murders and going over old case files. Of all the hundreds of corpses I've seen, only one body has ever looked the way this one did. And that was James Arkel."

It felt like the temperature in the room had dropped by a couple of degrees. Carnegie sighed and rubbed his eyes, while Lucien bit a fingernail pensively. Arthur looked regretful for even having mentioned the name.

"Sorry, but who's James Arkel?" asked Jonathan.

"Good question," an amused voice answered from the doorway. "You should be a reporter."

A boy was leaning idly against the door frame, hands in his pockets. His sleeves were rolled up, and a couple of shirt buttons left undone, in order to display as much of his muscular physique as possible. Despite looking the same age as Jonathan, he carried himself with an easy arrogance, and his voice dripped with condescension.

"Harry Pierce, I've told you a million times to knock before coming in here," Lucien said sharply. "This isn't a good time."

"Sorry, boss. But come on — he's got to be the only person in Darkside who doesn't know who James Arkel is. We could put him on the 'Believe It or Not!' page in tonight's edition!"

"I'm not from around here," Jonathan shot back coldly.

"Well, let me fill you in." Harry pulled up a chair before anyone could stop him. "James Arkel is the most famous murder victim in the history of Darkside — and you'd better believe there's been a fair bit of competition for *that* title. Twelve years ago he was found dead on the roof of the Cain Club — and however he'd died, it hadn't been pretty. Anyway, word got out that this wasn't any old corpse, but the son of Thomas Ripper, grandson of Jack the Ripper, and the current ruler of Darkside — though for how much longer that old boy's going to stay around is another question . . ."

"Harry!" Arthur warned.

"Right. Sorry, boss. Anyway, Thomas was so furious that he tore the place apart trying to find out who was responsible, but the killer was never found. To this day no one knows who would dare try to kill a Ripper, and — more important — why. Was it a random murder? Or had someone managed to find out that James was a Ripper before the Blood Succession?"

"Blood Succession? What's that?"

Harry laughed disbelievingly. "Another searching question about the obvious. Is there anything you *do* know?"

"That'll do, Pierce," Lucien cut in. "I think you've graced us with enough of your presence for one day. And stop eavesdropping!"

The boy bowed mockingly, and withdrew.

"Sorry about that," Lucien said apologetically. "I should really fire that brat. Problem is, he's got the makings of a fine reporter. We can't afford to be picky around here. The staff gets smaller every day." He looked at Carnegie. "But you understand why we're taking this case so seriously. It may be nothing, but if there's even the slightest link to James's murder, then it's worth the effort. What do you say?"

"You know my usual rates?"

Lucien smiled. "Your reputation precedes you. And I wouldn't dream of offering anything less."

Carnegie picked at his teeth with a claw, and spat something on the floor. "You've got yourself a deal, then. Enough jabbering. Come on, boy, we need to go and find out who this guy is."

"And how exactly are we going to do that?" Jonathan asked sourly. What with arguing with Carnegie and now Harry rubbing him the wrong way, he felt distinctly at odds with the world.

The wereman ignored the tone in his voice and addressed the room. "Well, we may not know who he is yet, but we know where he's been. Right?"

Jonathan shrugged, while Lucien and Arthur waited expectantly.

Carnegie shook his head. "I don't know. Reporters! What did you say you'd found on the body again?"

"Erm . . . keys, coins, and . . . oh, I see."

Arthur pulled out a slim white box of matches. On the front, the phrase THE MIDNIGHT had been printed in black lettering.

"We'll start there, then, shall we?"

The Informer's star reporter looked thoughtfully at the wereman. "I think I should come with you. If you're going to stumble across some sort of exclusive, I want to be there."

Carnegie shrugged. "It's your money. Just make sure you don't get in my way. Come on, then."

They were halfway down the stairs back to the main office when a thought occurred to Jonathan. He tugged on Arthur's sleeve. "Before we go, can you show me where my mom worked?"

The reporter nodded sympathetically. "Of course. Follow me."

He led Jonathan over to a quiet part of the office, where a desk lay untouched. Had the windows not been boarded up, it would have looked out over the streets beyond and back toward the Grand. Even though the chair was vacant, someone had lit a candle nearby, casting a gentle light over inkwells and pots filled with fountain pens. A thick ledger was open on the desk, and Jonathan could see graceful handwriting flowing across the page like the tide.

"We've left her things as they were," Arthur explained. "It just didn't feel right letting anyone else work here. I know it's been twelve years, but I still hope that one day she might come back."

Jonathan settled into the chair, and with a trembling hand flicked through the heavy book. Until now, one solitary photo had been the only link he had to his mom. But she had sat in this chair and she had written in this ledger. He opened a drawer in the desk, and his heart raced to see that it was filled with notebooks. There was so much he had to read, so much he had to learn.

"Come on, boy," Carnegie said, not unkindly. "You can come back and look over her things later. Let's go and see what we can find out."

He placed a large hand on Jonathan's shoulder, and the two of them turned to go, with Arthur stomping along in their wake. From the other side of the office, Harry Pierce watched them leave, his eyes glinting in the candlelight.

5

Carnegie hailed a hansom cab outside the offices of *The Informer*, and they headed back toward the center of Darkside. The mild sunshine of earlier had been smothered behind frowning black clouds. Rain was pattering on the roof of the carriage. Inside, Arthur scribbled into a notebook, which looked child-sized in his chubby grasp.

Jonathan stared moodily out of the window at the damp world outside. Beside him, Carnegie had tilted his hat over his eyes and was lying back against the seat snoring, mouth wide open. A thin line of dribble was running down his chin. Despite all that the wereman had done for him, Jonathan couldn't shake off a feeling of resentment toward Carnegie. He had been hiding things about Theresa, just like Alain. Why was everyone so reluctant to tell Jonathan about his mom? It made his blood boil to think about it. Worse than that, it confirmed what he had always thought before arriving in Darkside: He had no friends. Everyone was hiding secrets. No one was to be trusted.

Still, he had learned one important thing: James Arkel had been murdered twelve years ago — the same year that his mother had vanished. Jonathan didn't know if there was a connection, but he was determined to find out.

"Arthur?"

The reporter looked up from his notebook.

"What was Harry talking about back there in the office? What's the Blood Succession?"

Digging into the pockets of his voluminous coat, Arthur pulled out a battered pamphlet and tossed it over to Jonathan.

"I thought you might ask me that, so I grabbed this before we left the office. After all, we can't have young Pierce lording it over you! This is short, but it's adequately written and should give you all the basic information."

The pamphlet consisted of a few sheets of paper pressed together beneath a purple cover. Jonathan glanced at the title, "The Ripper Bloodline," and couldn't help noticing it had been written by one A. Blake. He opened it and began to read:

If someone wishes to follow the twisted branches of the Ripper family tree, they must first learn about the Blood Succession, the rite of passage that determines each ruler of Darkside. The Blood Succession was initiated under Darkside's first ruler, Jack, who in his diabolical wisdom decreed that his children should fight to the death to determine who was the worthiest heir.

Victory could be sought by any means, fair or foul, as long as one rule was respected: The battle was to take place on Lightside, after Jack's death. This was meant to remind the new ruler of Darkside's origins, and of the weak-minded and fearful Lightsiders who had originally banished them from the rest of London.

To prevent the eruption of all-out war taking place before his demise, Jack further decreed that his heirs must live in Darkside under assumed names, and swear to hide their true identities until the day of Succession.

In this manner, when Jack finally passed away at the age of seventy-seven, his sons George and Albert revealed themselves, and traveled to Lightside to fight. At that time a great war was raging in London, and both Rippers nearly died in a bombing raid. However, George survived and returned to take his place on the Darkside throne.

Thirty years later, Thomas succeeded his father after surviving a chaotic four-way battle that left him at death's door for several days. Since that time, however, his iron-fisted rule has only served to prove the worth of the Blood Succession.

The rain was coming down more heavily now. The carriage had turned onto the Grand, where the sidewalks were more crowded and raucous. Distracted by the garish costumes and the foul-mouthed arguments, Jonathan folded up the pamphlet and stuck it in his back pocket.

The Midnight was situated in the basement of a large

building on the north side of the Grand. Its entrance was hidden away behind a wrought-iron railing and down a flight of stone steps. The casual passerby would have no idea it was there, and that was just the way the patrons of the Midnight liked it.

As the hansom cab came to a halt, Carnegie pushed up his hat and glanced around, instantly awake. He bounded out of the cab and tossed a couple of coins to the driver.

"Keep the change," he barked.

The driver glanced at the meager tip and made as if to say something in retort, but took one look at the hulking form of the private detective and seemed to think better of it. Instead, he gee'd up his horse and galloped away down the Grand.

As they started down the steps, Carnegie placed a warning hand on Jonathan's shoulders. "It's pitch-black in here. You're not going to be able to see a thing, which means you'll have to rely on me to keep an eye out for you. One thing wolves don't have a problem with is the dark. So sit tight, leave the talking to me, and try not to get into any trouble, OK?"

Jonathan nodded sullenly.

"Good. Let's go."

At the bottom of the steps was a thick wooden door next to a copper plaque bearing the pub's name. Through the entrance was a hallway leading to another door, which refused to open until Arthur closed the outer door behind them, plunging them into darkness. Jonathan felt his heartbeat quicken.

"They have to make sure no sunlight gets in," breathed Carnegie. "Down here, people's eyes get so accustomed to the dark that even the slightest ray of light could blind them. Ready?"

He pushed open the door, and they entered the Midnight. The darkness was immediate and total. Jonathan couldn't even make out the vague outline of shapes around him. He was utterly blind. He walked slowly and cautiously forward, arms outstretched like a sleep-walker. Stripped of his sight, he had to fall back on his other senses to paint a picture of his surroundings. The smell was overpowering: a curdling odor of beer and unwashed armpits. His ears picked up a subdued murmur of conversation, the occasional clink of a glass or a glug of liquid from a bottle, the scrape of a chair leg across the floor.

A hand clutched Jonathan's arm. He jumped with shock.

"Easy, boy. It's only me. I'm going to lead you over to a table where I can leave you. I want to talk to the bartender."

"Where's Arthur?"

"About to crash into the bar. I'll get him in a minute."

"What does this place look like?"

"Put it this way, boy. I know why they keep the lights off. Now, come on."

Jonathan allowed himself to be led over to what he presumed to be a quiet corner of the room. Despite Carnegie's guidance, he still managed to trip over the foot of a hidden drinker, eliciting a hiss of displeasure from out of the darkness. He felt safer when he was seated, especially when he heard Arthur's voice getting nearer.

"Look," he was protesting. "If we're going to have to hang around in this dungeon, you might as well let me get a drink."

"No time," came Carnegie's growled response. "I don't want to spend any longer here than we have to. Now sit."

Jonathan heard the sizable thump next to him as

Arthur was forced down into his chair, and then the sound of footsteps padding away from them.

The reporter drummed his fingers on the surface of the table. "This place leaves a lot to be desired," he muttered.

"You feeling nervous too?" Jonathan whispered back.

"I'd feel a lot happier if I knew where the nearest exit was. I always make sure I know that when I enter any building. I've tried to memorize my steps back to the front door here, but I wouldn't like to put it to the test."

"Me neither."

The table fell silent again. While his vision remained nonexistent, Jonathan was convinced that his hearing was already becoming sharper and more discerning. Straining his ears, he could just about make out Carnegie's gruff undertone at the bar. There must have been a table nearby, because he could hear the long gulps of someone drinking, and the satisfied sigh that followed each gulp. Somewhere to his left, he could hear two men talking nervously. Jonathan leaned forward and tried to eavesdrop.

". . . it's true, I tell you. I heard it from a butler who works for the Ripper. Thomas hasn't got long left. Months at best."

"It's not that surprising. He must be getting a bit old."

"Still, it's not good news. I'd be surprised if any of his kids turn out to be as strong as Thomas. Born ruler, he is. They figured that James might have turned out to be his father's equal, but look what happened to him. It was a black day for Darkside the day he was murdered, I tell you."

"Keep your voice down! You never know who's listening . . ."

And with that, the volume of their conversation dipped below Jonathan's hearing. He sighed and sat back. The novelty value of the Midnight was rapidly wearing thin. He was grateful when he heard Carnegie padding back toward them. A hand brushed his arm.

"How did it go?" Jonathan asked cheerily.

"Shut up, you piece of filth."

The voice was not Carnegie's. Jonathan would have cried out, but he could feel the chill of a blade nestling against his throat. A dull thud next to him was followed by a groan from Arthur. An unshaven face pressed close to his. When he spoke, his assailant's breath was heavily, but not unpleasantly, spiced.

"All alone now. Who's going to help you?"

Jonathan started to reply, only to feel the blade pressing more tightly against his throat.

"No need to shout," the attacker said soothingly. "We can have a very quiet chat, just the two of us."

"What . . . what do you want?"

"I want to know what you're doing here. Sitting next to a reporter. Your friend — a private detective, if my eyes don't deceive me — asking questions at the bar. Personal questions."

"You can see?" Jonathan gasped.

The man chuckled. "Oh yes . . . I see everything."

From over by the bar there came a howl of rage, and Jonathan guessed that Carnegie's wolf-eyes had spotted what was going on. His attacker tensed, wrapping his arm around Jonathan's neck like a vise. Just breathing was a struggle.

"Better stay very still," the man whispered. "I'd hate to slip."

From Jonathan's left came the sound of rapidly approaching footsteps, and the sound of breathing. Not the regular exhalations of a human, but the ragged pants of an enraged predator.

"That's close enough, Carnegie."

"Correlli? What are *you* doing here?"

"I could ask you the same question. You shouldn't be walking around here asking questions, poking your nose in matters that don't concern you. It makes people nervous."

"People get nervous when they do bad things," replied the wereman. "What bad things have you done?"

"Too many to count, my friend. And I'll do more before I rot."

"Did you do anything bad to Edwin Rafferty?"

Correlli's arm stiffened, squeezing a cry of pain from Jonathan. "I'll kill the boy. Don't doubt that."

"I don't. But if he dies, then I'll rip you apart and eat you. Don't doubt that, either."

The man chuckled again. It was as if he was enjoying himself. "Very well, my friend. When you are in unimaginable torment, and only seconds from death, do remember that I gave you this warning: Stop asking questions — about Edwin Rafferty, about *anything* — or you will suffer the highest price. Let me enlighten you."

Jonathan felt the arm loosen from around his neck. There was a flick of a match as it sparked into life. Squinting against the sudden light, Jonathan could see a huge man, shirtless underneath a red waistcoat, raising a flaming brand to his lips. Suddenly there was a roar, and the man breathed tongues of flames across the room. The light was piercingly bright, and men who hadn't seen the glare of the sun for months screamed as the brilliance singed their dilated pupils. Jonathan bunched his eyes shut, and felt himself flying sideways as his assailant cast him to one side. His head cracked against the cold stone floor. There was another roar, and more screams from the patrons of the Midnight. Panicky footsteps careered across the floor as blind men struggled to find the exit. His head swimming from the impact and the smell of burning in his nostrils, Jonathan thought he heard Carnegie bellow with pain, and then there was nothing.

6

Nicholas de Quincy strode through the door of a greasy café in Finsbury Park and banged it shut behind him, making the waitress jump and earning a glare from the cook behind the counter. De Quincy ignored him. The long journey from Darkside to this part of North London had put him in a foul mood, and the sight of the café had only made things worse. This, he seethed, was the last time that he would allow Humphrey to choose the meeting place.

He rubbed his monocle on a black handkerchief and peered around the dingy café. The air was thick with the smell of fried food and the windows damp with condensation. Tinny music crackled out from a radio. It was late morning, and the green plastic chairs were empty save for one corner table, where Humphrey Granville was leading a ferocious assault on a huge pile of sausage, bacon, eggs, and baked beans. Rounds of toast were stacked high on a side plate, alongside a steaming cup of coffee. As de Quincy watched, Humphrey broke from his food to take a loud slurp, dousing his mustache in the hot liquid. A newspaper was spread out in front of him on the Formica table. Engrossed in his reading, Humphrey didn't notice the beans spilling down his jacket as he shoveled them into his mouth.

De Quincy removed his top hat and ran a hand through his stiff, spiky hair in an attempt to collect himself. Then he made his way over to the table and squeezed his long frame into a seat.

"Granville," he said, in a voice several degrees below freezing.

Humphrey's broad face broke into a smile. "Nicholas! You made it!"

"No thanks to your directions. Why on Darkside did you make us meet in this pigsty?"

His voice echoed around the deserted café. Humphrey winced.

"I do wish you'd keep your voice down when you say things like that, Nicholas. It tends to get people's backs up. Try the food." He waved at his fast-emptying plate. "It's the finest fry-up in all of London, and they serve an uncommonly good portion."

"I'm not hungry," came the icy reply. "Can't you keep your mind off your belly for one minute, you stupid man?"

Glancing around, de Quincy caught sight of the waitress hovering uncertainly nearby.

"Coffee," he ordered curtly, and then turned back toward Granville, who was glumly mopping up the final streaks of yolk and ketchup with a piece of toast. De Quincy pointed at the newspaper. "Taking a sudden interest in world events, are we?"

Humphrey shook his head. "It's an old *Informer*. I kept this one for . . . obvious reasons."

He pushed the aging newspaper toward de Quincy, who cast an eye over the front page. Immediately he recognized it. All Darksiders remembered this story.

"THE ONLY INFORMER YOU CAN TRUST"

RIPPER'S SON SLAIN!

BY ARTHUR BLAKE

Darkside was in a state of shock today following the announcement that James Arkel, murdered president of the Cain Club, was in fact the son of Thomas Ripper, grand ruler of the borough. Arkel's savaged body was discovered by a young kitchen hand on the roof of the private-members' establishment two nights ago. He had been a prominent and popular figure in Darkside society, and news of his death was initially greeted with incredulity by the wealthiest men in the borough. And now, with the revelation of his true identity, the shock waves have spread to the ordinary men and women in the street. For the first time in Darkside history, a Ripper heir has been murdered before the Blood Succession.

Speculation is rife as to the motive for the killing. Was it simply a random attack, or had Arkel's reputation and standing made him a target for jealous rivals? Another, darker rumor flying around the drinking dens

of Darkside is that Arkel was murdered because some-
one had uncovered his true identity.

What is certain is that the Rippers' private force
of Bow Street Runners are conducting an investiga-
tion that is unprecedented in its scale and violence.
In just forty-eight hours over a hundred Darksiders
have been brought in for questioning: As yet, none
have been released. One officer said, "Thomas will
do whatever it takes to catch his son's killer. He'll tear
apart the foundations of Darkside if necessary. No one
is safe."

Sources close to the Ripper have confirmed that there
are now only two heirs left to contest the Blood
Succession. Their identities and whereabouts remain
the most closely guarded of secrets.

"Sensational stuff," de Quincy remarked mildly, tossing the newspaper back to Granville. "I hardly need reminding of the details, though. After all, we were the ones who did it."

Humphrey waved his arms in a shushing gesture. "Keep your voice down, man!"

"I think we're probably safe. Even a Bow Street Runner wouldn't be crazy enough to eat here."

"This is no joke, Nicholas!" Humphrey paused as the waitress returned, placing a cup before de Quincy. When she had gone, he resumed speaking in a hushed whisper. "I'll admit that we were the ones who lured him up onto the roof. But we didn't know he was going to be torn to pieces up there! We didn't know he was a Ripper!"

"Well, we knew that Arkel wasn't going to come back *down* from the roof, and it was unlikely he was going to be tickled to death. If you are going to be so squeamish about this, Granville, you should never have gotten involved in the first place."

Humphrey drew himself up in his seat proudly. "Brother Fleet asked for our assistance in disposing of Arkel. We were all Gentlemen — the elite of the Cain Club. We were obliged to help!"

"I suppose there was that," de Quincy mused. "I simply thought it would be fun. And it gave me a hold over Brother Fleet that I thought might come in handy later on. Of course, it turned out to be an even bigger hold than I could have dreamed of. When we found out that he was a Ripper, too, and that he had killed his own brother . . ." His thin lips twisted into a smile. "Well, it was like all my birthdays rolled into one. Which brings us neatly back to the present, and our current business."

A pensive look crossed Humphrey's face, and he took a nervous sip of his coffee. "Look, you may be happy, Nicholas, but I'm worried. When I agreed to help you with this scheme, you promised me that there was no way we could get hurt."

De Quincy's eyes narrowed. "You look well enough to me."

"But after what happened to poor Edwin . . ."

"After what?"

"Haven't you heard, Nicholas? They found his body in an alleyway yesterday."

"Oh."

"Is that all you have to say? Don't you understand? Edwin's dead! Word is he was murdered!"

De Quincy took a sip of his coffee, winced, and pushed it to one side. "Look, if no one else had killed Edwin Rafferty, I would have done it myself."

"Nicholas!" Humphrey cried, shocked.

"Face facts, Granville. The man was a walking liability. Who knows how much he's drunkenly blabbed in the Midnight? We should never have included him in the first place."

"But he was one of us! He was a *Gentleman*!"

De Quincy grimaced. "I would have thought that recent events would have proved to you that the Gentlemen don't exist anymore. It's just me and you, Granville."

"But if they can kill Edwin, who's to say they can't kill us?"

The blackmailer snorted. "I wouldn't worry just yet. We don't know *what* happened to Rafferty. Maybe he tripped over his own shoelaces and banged his head. And if it was one of the Rippers, so what? It's a warning shot, nothing more. Rafferty was little more than a bargaining chip."

Humphrey looked down at his plate. "I suppose you'd have said the same thing if I'd been the one who was murdered."

"Come, come, Granville," de Quincy said, patting him with a bone-cold hand. "I told you. It's just me and you now. We have to stick together. Look, the plan is progressing exactly as it should. We have contacted both of the Ripper's remaining children — our old friend Brother Fleet, and Marianne. They are now keenly aware that we know their assumed identities, and will happily divulge this information to whoever pays us the most money. Now let's see how high we can drive the auction."

"Do you think they'll pay?"

De Quincy bit back an oath. "Granville, we're offering them a passport to the Ripper's throne. No Blood Succession, no risk of a painful death. All they have to do is bump off the other in some dingy corner of Darkside, and wait until dear old Thomas dies. They'll pay, all right. For pity's sake, hold your nerve. Within a week this will all be over, and you'll be one of the richest men in Darkside." He rose, fitting his top hat over his stiff hair. "Time to leave this wretched hovel. Are you coming?"

Humphrey shook his head vigorously. "After what happened to Edwin? No fear. Darkside's too dangerous right now. I'm not going back until this deal is done and dusted."

"As you wish." De Quincy looked around pointedly. "Though for the life of me I can't understand how you can spend time in Lightside."

"Oh, if you'd only try it," Humphrey replied, his eyes suddenly shining, "you'd see that there's so much to do. Everywhere I go, every street I walk down, I see these beautiful restaurants, menus crammed with dishes we've never even heard of. Do you know what curry is, Nicholas? Or chicken chow mein?"

De Quincy shook his head.

"Every mouthful is an experience here. And even if I dined out every day, it would take me years to eat in all the restaurants here."

Humphrey sat back in his chair with a dreamy smile. Not trusting himself to say something pleasant, de Quincy nodded stiffly and hurried out the door. Seeing that the coast was clear, the waitress returned to the table and began clearing the plates.

"Anything else?" she inquired.

Humphrey checked his pocket watch and glanced up at the menu board. It wasn't as if there was anything important he had to do today.

"I'll have the same meal again, please. With mushrooms this time, I think."

As the waitress bustled back toward the counter he unfolded the ancient copy of *The Informer* and began to read the front page again.

7

They fought the blaze through the night and into the dawn, ranks of Darksiders passing buckets of water in human chains. As the fire spread outward from the Midnight and dragged the rest of the building into its furious embrace, it seemed like a hopeless task. Men had to bellow at one another to make themselves heard above the roar. Flames danced in the sky above the Grand.

Gradually, however, the Darksiders began to get the upper hand. They attached hosepipes to fire hydrants in the street, and sent streams of water into the heart of the blaze. Wounded, the fire pawed at the woodwork and lashed out at anyone foolish enough to get too close. But by the time the bleary sun had risen into the sky, the last flames were being extinguished.

It was far too late for the Midnight, though. The pub was a blackened shell belching smoke rings from its interior. No longer would anyone be able to descend the steps and hide away from the world in the pitch-black. A group of regulars milled around outside, in the dazed hope that somehow it would reopen in a few minutes.

On the sidewalk on the other side of the street, Jonathan winced as another bolt of pain jarred his skull. He felt dreadful. Being knocked out twice in a matter of hours was clearly not good for him. He rubbed the bump on his head, and looked around as the Grand returned to something like normality.

"I'm surprised anyone bothered to put the fire out," he said.

"Self-preservation, boy."

Carnegie's clothes were singed, and his face blackened with soot. He was down on his haunches next to Jonathan, the prone bulk of Arthur Blake between them. He paused as a thick cough burst up from his lungs, and then continued.

"If the Midnight goes up in flames, maybe another building follows — next thing you know, the Grand's burned down, and so has your house. Fire's everybody's enemy."

"Even so, I'm surprised."

"Darksiders might be a bad bunch, but we're not stupid."

There was a protracted groan, and then Arthur heaved himself up. An ugly bruise was swelling on his temple. "What happened?" he asked groggily.

"We got jumped by a man called Correlli," replied Carnegie. "He's a hired hand. I've had enough run-ins with him in the past to know that he's one of the toughest characters in the borough. You really don't want to mess with him. Anyway, he torched the place and ran. I managed to drag you and the boy out before the place burned down. Nearly got barbecued in the process, mind you."

"What did he want?"

"Just your standard threat — 'stay away or else.' I've had hundreds of them. Correlli doesn't come cheap, though. Someone really doesn't want us investigating this case."

Jonathan frowned, remembering something. "Who's Edwin Rafferty?"

"Eh?"

"You mentioned him back in the Midnight."

Carnegie scratched vigorously behind his ear. "Oh, right. I asked one of the barmen if he'd noticed anything unusual in the past day or so. The only thing he could think of was that he hadn't seen Rafferty — and apparently it was very rare he *wasn't* in the Midnight. So I thought I'd bring it up with our friend back there, see if it got a reaction. I think we struck lucky."

"It didn't feel very lucky at the time." Jonathan rubbed his head.

Carnegie chuckled. "Being a private detective isn't all fun and games, you know." He turned to Arthur. "Does Rafferty mean what I think it does?"

The reporter nodded.

"Money. And lots of it."

Several hours later, his head still pounding, Jonathan found himself standing in a cramped terraced street in the Lower Fleet, where residents listened through paper-thin walls to their neighbors bickering and quarreling. Dirty puddles swamped the cobblestones. The sky was stained with acrid smoke. Edwin Rafferty resided in a particularly grim dwelling underneath a railway bridge, and every few minutes his house winced as a train rattled overhead. The windows were coated in a thick film of grime, while the front door was hanging off its hinges. Even in the depths of the Lower Fleet, the building emanated squalor.

"I don't get it. I thought you said this guy was rich?" Jonathan said.

"His family is," Arthur replied. "One of the oldest and most disreputable families in Darkside, the Raffertys. Made an absolute fortune from smuggling."

"What went wrong?"

"Edwin went wrong. He spent more time in pubs than on boats. His family got so sick of him drinking away their fortune that they disinherited him. Shall we go inside?"

Carnegie eyed the open doorway. "Sure. Do you want to knock, or shall I?"

He loped forward and pushed the door, which promptly broke open and landed with a crash on the hallway floor. Carnegie shook his head, and went in.

Entering Edwin Rafferty's house was like stepping inside a giant coffin. There was a musty odor of decay and neglect that hinted at years of joyless solitude. The interior was eerily empty. In the front room, a rocking chair lay still, a glass of murky liquid on the table next to it. There were no other pieces of furniture in the room. The whitewashed walls were coated in grime, but there were no pictures or paintings hanging from them. Carnegie's footsteps echoed on the wooden floorboards.

The story was the same throughout the house. In the kitchen, a rusty tap dribbled water into the sink. The cupboards were bare, and there was no evidence that food had ever been prepared there. Up the stairs there was a bedroom containing just a bed, mirror, and washstand. Down the hall, a breeze whipped through the broken window into a completely empty room.

"No wonder he spent all his time in the Midnight," said Jonathan. "There's not much to do here, is there?"

"Not many leads, either," Arthur replied.

Carnegie stopped in his tracks and frowned. "There's something that doesn't add up."

"What?"

"Remember what Rafferty had in his pockets? The front door's hanging off the hinges, and there's nothing in the house. What did he need a key for?"

Arthur's eyes lit up. "He kept something locked up. I bet there's a safe hidden around here somewhere!"

They set to work immediately, exploring every inch of the house, rifling cupboards and turning over furniture.

They disturbed flies and spiders and earned a series of high-pitched rebukes from nesting rats, but couldn't find any safe. After an hour of fruitless searching in the kitchen, Jonathan went upstairs and found Carnegie slumped on the broken bed, staring at his reflection in Rafferty's grubby mirror.

"I don't get it," the wereman said. "There's nothing in this wretched house. Where could he have hidden anything?"

A dispirited figure appeared in the doorway, covered in black powder.

"Anything up the chimney, Arthur?"

The reporter shook his head, and sneezed violently. "Only soot."

"You've got to hand it to Rafferty. He may not have been much to look at, but he wasn't completely stupid."

"That's it!" Jonathan cried out.

"What's it?"

"You said Rafferty was a drunk and a slob, right? So he didn't really care about his appearance?"

Carnegie smiled thinly. "You could say that, yes."

Jonathan turned and looked pointedly at the mirror. "So he wouldn't have been arranging his hair in that."

"Good thinking, boy."

The wereman sprang up and went over to the wash-stand, tracing a finger around the edge of the mirror. Apparently deep in thought, he tore off a long strip of bed linen and wrapped it around a clublike fist.

"You're not going to smash it, are you?" Jonathan inquired. "That's seven years' bad luck, you know."

Carnegie chuckled. "It can't be any worse than hanging around you, boy. You're a walking bad omen. And anyway, if there's some sort of trigger mechanism, it's cleverer than I am. Now stand back, and cover your eyes."

His fist flew through the air and crashed into the mirror, which exploded into a thousand shards of glass. Satisfied, the wereman brushed away the final remaining pieces, revealing a plain metal safe behind. He removed the linen from his hand, and gingerly rubbed his knuckles.

"That's going to hurt for a while." Carnegie turned to Jonathan. "Good work there, boy. You get to unwrap the present. Arthur — you still got the key on you?"

Arthur nodded, and eagerly handed it to Jonathan. The key slipped into the lock and turned with surprising ease. A large bound book was inside. Opening it up, Jonathan was surprised to see each page was filled with rough sketches and drawings of people and famous buildings in Darkside.

"Seems Edwin thought of himself as an artist," he said.

Laying the sketchbook down on the bed, he gingerly fished around for what was left in the safe. His hand settled on an envelope at the back. Long since opened, it contained a letter written on faded notepaper:

21.I.DY106

BROTHER SPINE,

I AM IN DESPERATE NEED OF YOUR ASSISTANCE. I HAVE BECOME ENMESHED IN A DIRE SCHEME THAT MAY WELL COST ME MY LIFE. IN MY HOUR OF NEED, I AM THROWING MYSELF ON THE MERCY OF THE GENTLEMEN, IN THE HOPE THAT THEY WILL HELP ME. MEET ME AT THE CLUB AT THE USUAL TIME TOMORROW NIGHT,

BROTHER FLEET

"This could be anything," murmured Jonathan. "What are those numbers across the top of the page?"

"The date," replied Carnegie. "The twenty-first of January, DarkYear 106."

Arthur smiled grimly. "I'm not surprised Correlli's threatening us. That's three days before James Ripper was murdered and, by the sound of it, Edwin was in on the plan."

8

An unholy silence reigned over the grounds of Vendetta Heights. Life had fled: No animals sniffed and scurried through the undergrowth, no birds wheeled and flocked over the estate. The onset of winter had drained the color from the trees: Only the hedgerows of the labyrinth in the center of the garden had managed to cling on to their dark leaves. Bare branches made anguished clenches at gray skies.

Down on the terrace, a group of workmen were inspecting the shattered remnants of a greenhouse. Affected by the unnatural stillness of the atmosphere, they crept around the shattered windowpanes, whispering nervously in one another's ears. The youngest of the group could barely keep still, his head darting this way and that at every imagined noise.

A makeshift canopy had been erected on the patio up by the mansion, from under which two figures watched the men at work. One was a young woman with flaming red hair, who stood attentively by the side of a wicker chair. In the chair sat a pale, blond man, a cane resting across his knee. His eyes burned with hatred. Vendetta: banker, vampire, the richest man in Darkside. When he spoke his voice was ragged.

"Remind me again, Raquella, why you decided to hire these oafs?"

There was a delicate pause as the maid weighed her response.

"Your reputation precedes you, sir. Finding workmen is not always easy."

"I'm sure you offered enough of my money to make it an attractive proposition."

"Most people refused to speak to me — no matter how much I offered them."

The vampire shifted restlessly in his chair. "I simply can't believe this rabble was all you could find."

"I did my best, sir," she replied implacably.

Snarling, Vendetta reached up and grabbed Raquella by the back of the neck, pulling her head down until she was level with his eyeline.

"This is all your fault. The workmen . . . the greenhouse . . . I should have drained you a long time ago. I know what you did. I know you helped the Starling boy. You betrayed me, and now look at me. *Look at me!*"

Raquella forced herself to meet his gaze. The vampire's skin, always pale, had now assumed an utterly lifeless pallor, and his cheeks were hollow. She remembered the night she had discovered him dragging himself up the steps of Vendetta Heights, blood pouring from a wound in his side. During a fight with Jonathan his own knife had been turned upon him. Most blades would have barely scratched him, but Vendetta's knife was coated with a rare substance that prevented his victims from passing on any infections through their blood. The overdose of this substance in his bloodstream had left him in agony.

Could a vampire — a creature of the undead — die? Raquella didn't know, but for the next few days Vendetta had come as close to mortality as she had ever seen him. Racked with a fever, he tossed and turned in bed, muttering phrases in a strange language. The slightest sliver of light caused him such pain that his screams echoed down the hallways of his enormous mansion.

Throughout the darkest days of Vendetta's illness, there had only been one person there to look after him. One person who had wiped the perspiration from his skin, tried to feed him food and water, wrenched open the windows when it was safely dark outside, and chased the stench of death from the stuffy bedroom. One person who, during one particularly long and painful night, had rolled up her shirtsleeve and pricked her arm with a sewing needle, allowing drops of blood to trickle into Vendetta's grateful mouth.

Raquella didn't know why she hadn't walked out that night and left her master to rot. Maybe she was so used to serving him that she didn't know anything else. In a strange way, did she feel guilty for betraying this brutal, evil man? Whatever the reason, her ministrations were probably the only thing that had stopped him from killing her. For now.

"You're hurting me," Raquella said through gritted teeth.

"You want to tell me about pain? I'm a cripple!"

The icy blast of his breath swept her face.

"You're getting stronger each day. It won't be long before you're walking again."

Vendetta let go of her neck. As she stumbled away from him, a series of hacking coughs rent his body.

"Need . . . to feed. Tell one of the guards to bring me a workman. The young one. He mustn't be able to struggle . . . I'm . . . so very weak . . ."

Smoothing her hair down, Raquella helped her master quietly back inside.

As dusk fell an exhausted Vendetta slept. He looked a little better for feeding; a hint of color had returned to his cheeks. The remaining workmen had fled, and wouldn't be returning. At this rate the greenhouse would never be repaired.

When she was satisfied that he was comfortable, Raquella pulled a heavy coat over her maid's outfit and slipped out of the side door into the gloomy evening. She walked quickly down the driveway, her footsteps crunching on the gravel. A shadowy figure opened the front gates for her: As always, she nodded in thanks, but avoided eye contact.

The wind was rummaging through the huge trees that lined Savage Row. Raquella found the sound strangely comforting. It was nice to be out in the fresh air. Usually she spent her nights in the cramped servants' quarters at Vendetta Heights, but tonight she had promised to visit her family down in the Lower Fleet. At the thought of seeing her parents and her brothers and sisters again, her footsteps instinctively quickened. Raquella would have liked to have saved time by taking a train on the Dark Line, but she was saving every penny. Her wages were the main reason her family could eat but, given Vendetta's current mood, she couldn't be sure how much longer she would be working. Or, for that matter, how much longer she was going to remain alive.

As Raquella headed past a giant mansion belonging to Darkside's most successful gambler, she heard the sound of a pebble skittering across the sidewalk on the other side of the street. She stopped and turned. A woman dressed in a flowing maroon cloak was standing underneath a streetlamp. Her fluorescent bright blue hair shone brilliantly in the soft light.

"Hello, Raquella," said Marianne. And smiled.

Tensing, the maidservant crossed the street. "Good evening, Marianne. You're getting lax. I heard you."

"If I had wanted to remain silent, you wouldn't have. I was merely being polite." Her eyes glinted. "Wouldn't want to *scare* you."

Raquella took an involuntary step back, bringing forth a peal of laughter from the bounty hunter.

"Oh, do come on. I merely wanted to pass on a message to one of your friends."

"Which friend?" Raquella asked suspiciously.

"The little one. Jonathan."

The maid looked startled. "I-I don't know anyone named Jonathan," she stammered.

"My dear, if you wanted to keep your friendship a secret, then perhaps you shouldn't have driven down the Grand with him in Vendetta's car. Did you think that no one noticed? Please don't play the innocent with me. You're too clever for that."

Raquella thought quickly. Having risked her life helping Jonathan take on Vendetta, she had resolved never to see him again. She had to admit to a small twinge of curiosity as to how the Lightsider was getting on, but there was no doubt her master would kill her if he knew she had spoken to Jonathan. Vendetta's patience stretched only so far. On the other hand, Marianne was very sharp, and extremely dangerous. Crossing her wasn't a good idea either.

"What's the message?"

"Firstly, let him know that I forgive him." She smiled coldly. "His actions hurt me, my reputation, and — worst of all — my pocket. But I am prepared to bury the hatchet, so to speak. There's no money in revenge, and anyway, I doubt that your master will be quite so . . . magnanimous when he recovers. Jonathan's going to be in quite enough trouble as it is."

Raquella shrugged. "If I run into him I'll pass it on. Anything else?"

"A little bird tells me people have been asking questions about the James Arkel murder. If they happen to get any answers, I want to hear about it." Marianne smiled again. "If I'm prepared to forgive him, it's the very least Jonathan can do for me. Got that?"

Raquella nodded, biting her lip.

"Excellent. Just in time."

A black carriage came clopping down Savage Row, driven by a giant, elongated figure. As it pulled up alongside them, a small, jittery man leapt out of the cab and held the door open for Marianne. A thought suddenly occurred to Raquella.

"Marianne?"

The bounty hunter inclined her head.

"Why are you doing this?"

Marianne smiled. "I always had a soft spot for the little one," she replied softly.

And with that, she swept up into the carriage. The small man followed her inside, and in a matter of moments the sounds of the horses had been swallowed up by the gloom. Raquella remained by the streetlamp, a thoughtful expression on her face.

It was pitch-black by the time she arrived at her parents' house, and immediately Raquella could tell that something was wrong. Her youngest brother, Daniel, was wandering outside in the street, crying. Raquella scooped him up into her arms.

"Danny? What's wrong?"

The little boy said nothing, merely pressed himself closer against his sister. The front door was ajar. Raquella entered the house slowly, her sense of foreboding growing. The lights were off and the hallway, usually a bright, bustling corridor filled with scampering children, was deserted.

"Ma?" she called out. "I found Danny outside. Where are you?"

There was no reply.

"Ma? Pa?"

Downstairs was empty. Raquella climbed the staircase, suddenly fearful of what she might find. At the end of the landing was her parents' cramped bedroom. Pushing the door open, Raquella saw her mother lying on the bed, head turned to one side, gazing out through the window at the streets beyond. Raquella's brothers and sisters were gathered around her, their faces creased with concern.

"What on Darkside's going on here? Where's Pa?"

There was a pause.

"He's gone," whispered her mother.

"Gone? Gone where?"

Without tearing her gaze from the window, her mother handed Raquella a note. The maidservant's hands shook as she read it.

MY DEAREST GEORGINA,

I HAVE ALWAYS FEARED THAT THIS DAY WOULD COME. FOR YEARS I HAVE BEEN KEEPING A DREADFUL SECRET. MANY NIGHTS I THOUGHT ABOUT TELLING YOU, BUT I KNEW THAT IT WOULD HAVE ONLY PUT YOU AND THE CHILDREN IN DANGER. NOW I KNOW THAT MY HOUR OF RECKONING HAS COME, AND I MUST FACE IT ALONE OR PLACE ALL THOSE I LOVE IN UNIMAGINABLE PERIL. A LIFE WITHOUT YOU IS BARELY A LIFE AT ALL, BUT I HOPE THAT IN TIME I SHALL BE ABLE TO RETURN TO YOU, MY LOVE. IN THE MEANWHILE, TAKE CARE OF ONE ANOTHER.

YOUR LOVING HUSBAND,

WILLIAM

"I . . . I don't understand," said Raquella. "What's this secret he's talking about? Where has he gone? What's going on, Ma?"

Georgina didn't reply to her daughter's question.

"Oh, my William," she whispered. "What have you done?"

9

A hansom cab came to a clattering halt outside the front door of the Rafferty house. Alerted by the noise, Jonathan, Carnegie, and Arthur headed outside in time to see Lucien Fox climbing awkwardly down from the carriage. The editor of *The Informer* hobbled toward Arthur, a testy expression etched on his face.

"This had better be good. You know I don't like to leave the office."

The reporter smiled grimly. "Oh, it's good, all right. In fact, it's so good that I didn't think it was a good idea advertising it around *The Informer*. You might trust your devoted staff, but I certainly don't."

They headed back into Edwin's glum front room, where the note from the safe had been left on the table. Lucien put on a pair of sharp-rimmed spectacles and began to inspect it thoroughly, the paper crackling under the touch of his fingers. He read the note several times in complete silence. Then he looked up, rubbing his neck thoughtfully.

"Well, it could be genuine," Lucien conceded. "Paper looks old enough."

Arthur beamed triumphantly, pressing the ever-present handkerchief to his perspiring forehead. "Unbelievable, isn't it? You know what this is, don't you? It's the first new clue to the James Ripper murder in over a decade!"

"I wouldn't get too carried away just yet," Lucien replied cautiously. "This note's only a couple of lines long, and it doesn't exactly prove anything. It could be referring to something else entirely."

"He's right," Carnegie sniffed. "This isn't adding up yet. Are you really suggesting that Darkside's most infamous murder was carried out by *Edwin Rafferty*? That man couldn't have organized a fistfight on the Grand."

Arthur frowned. "I know it could be nothing. But I've got the same sort of feeling I got when investigating the Claude du Pont murder. No one then thought the chimney sweep could have been responsible for such a fiendish act, but I soon showed them. When I get hunches, they don't tend to be wrong."

"That, at least, is true," Lucien acknowledged wryly. "But even if the note is something to do with James Ripper, where does it lead you? Ever heard of this Brother Fleet?"

"I can't say I have, but I can ask around. Someone on Darkside will know who he is . . ."

He was interrupted by Carnegie clearing his throat loudly.

"That's one way of doing it. It's a bit random, though. There is another approach we could try."

"What do you mean?"

"Look at the note again."

Both Lucien and Arthur peered closely at the small slip of paper, frowning with concentration. After a few seconds the editor clucked his tongue with frustration.

"I give in. What are we missing?"

"Bet you the boy spots it."

Arthur handed the note to Jonathan, who stared at it intently. Beneath the small, crabby handwriting, he could just about make out a faint pattern that was part of the paper itself.

"It's some kind of design . . ." he said. "Two letter 'C's wrapped around each other."

"Of course! A watermark!" cried Arthur.

"And which Darkside institution uses that particular design?"

The reporter thought for a second.

"Oh. Toffs," he said glumly.

They headed west, toward the far end of the Grand. The locals were in a particularly hostile mood that evening, and Jonathan was glad of Carnegie's baleful presence beside him as they moved along the pavement. Arthur and Lucien followed a pace behind. Though ostensibly in conversation, they paid little attention to each other. Instead their eyes flitted restlessly this way and that, on a permanent lookout for new scoops and exclusives.

As they passed Kinski's Theater of the Macabre, a scream ripped through the night. Jonathan turned to see a man being dragged by his heels through the doorway of the Aurora Borealis Exotic Candle Shop. Scrabbling frantically for something to cling on to, the man's hands fastened themselves around a lamppost. He didn't scream for help; he must have known there was no point. The tug-of-war lasted for a few seconds, until the unseen creature from inside the Aurora Borealis gave a final wrench, and the man flew into the dark recesses of the shop. All that remained was his top hat, rolling forlornly around the sidewalk.

"They must really want to sell him candles," Jonathan said.

"That's one way of looking at it," Carnegie conceded. "Either that, or they really want to make him *into* candles."

A look of horror flashed across Jonathan's face, making the wereman guffaw loudly.

"Darkside still shocks you, doesn't it? I'd have thought you'd have gotten used to it by now."

"There's a fair bit to get used to!" Jonathan replied indignantly. "It might help if everyone in this place wasn't so crazy!"

"Where would the fun be then? Come on, this way."

Beckoning, he turned off the Grand and down a wide, secluded road. The crescent moon was low in the sky, and it shone down on a row of large white Victorian-style townhouses. Carnegie headed toward the largest of the buildings, smugly enthroned at the end of the street. A terrace of semicircular steps flowed up to the ornate front door, which was flanked by a pair of enormous marble pillars. A coat of arms had been set above the doorway, with the Latin inscription EGO SUM MESSOR FRATRIS MEI. Curtains prevented the prying eyes of the poor and the unworthy from seeing what was happening inside the building. Two hulking men had been squeezed into doormen's liveries, the tassels and braids perching uncomfortably on two bodies built for — and sustained by — violence.

"There it is," said the wereman. "The Cain Club. The most exclusive private-members' club in Darkside. Only the filthy rich can get in."

Lucien coughed meaningfully. "On that point, now that we're here . . . how *do* you intend for us to get in? I'm guessing you're not a member?"

Carnegie eyed him narrowly. "My membership lapsed."

"Of course. It's just that the guards here aren't renowned for their amicable nature, and perhaps it would be wise to come up with a plan before we go any farther."

"OK. How about you shut up for a second and let me get on with it? You journalists talk too much."

The editor blanched.

Jonathan looked over his shoulder and smiled. "Carnegie's not renowned for his amicable nature either. If I were you, I'd follow his lead on this one."

As the wereman strode on, Lucien pulled Jonathan back and whispered in his ear, "Does he ever threaten you?"

"Most days."

"I can't claim to know him that well, but I'm more than aware of his reputation. Are you sure he's the sort of character you want to be associated with?"

Loping up the steps of the Cain Club, Carnegie didn't bother to say a word to either of the doormen as he brushed past them. Shocked by his disheveled appearance, they paused for a split second. It was enough. Carnegie lashed out with his left foot, kicking one of the doormen in the solar plexus and knocking him back against the pillar. The other doorman swung a clumsy fist, but the wereman ducked underneath its arc and kneed him sharply in the groin. Carnegie surveyed the slumped forms of the two men with mock surprise, and then turned and called back to his companions.

"Are you coming in, or what?"

Jonathan grinned at the editor. "Lucien, Carnegie's *exactly* the sort of character I want to be associated with."

They moved carefully past the doormen into a grand entrance hall. There was no one in sight, and Carnegie was already striding across the black-and-white checkered tiles toward a set of double doors at the end of the hall. Above the doors the sign read MAIN LOUNGE. Jonathan glanced pensively at Lucien and Arthur, and then the three of them hastened after the wereman.

There was a brittle civility to the main lounge of the Cain Club that Jonathan hadn't ever encountered in Darkside. Men in black evening suits milled around the vast room, talking and drinking together in small groups. Their faces were almost entirely obscured by black masks, twisted into the leering features of goblins and gargoyles. Plush armchairs and green potted plants were wreathed in thick cigar smoke. On the walls, exquisite watercolor paintings depicted scenes of graphic violence. From time to time a startling peal of laughter or the chink of crystal glasses rose above the general hubbub of conversation.

Heads turned at the sudden entrance of the unmasked and shabbily dressed arrivals. Jonathan couldn't see any expressions change beneath the masks, but could feel a sudden hostility chilling the heat rolling off the log fires. Beside him, Carnegie took great pleasure in beaming at the members, exposing his sharp canines.

Arthur tugged at his collar nervously. "What do we do now?" he hissed.

"We haven't got long until those doormen come back with some friends," Carnegie replied out of the corner of his mouth. "Let's split up and look around. See if you can find anything connected with Edwin Rafferty."

With that, the wereman barged off into the throng. Jonathan took one look at the members and headed back the way he had come. The entrance hall was still deserted. Keen to put some distance between himself and any recovering doormen, Jonathan raced up the staircase two steps at a time.

It didn't take many minutes of exploration upstairs before he came to the conclusion that the Cain Club was a huge rabbit warren. The upper levels were deserted, and Jonathan wandered through dining rooms and studies and billiard rooms without bumping into anybody.

Nevertheless, every room was lit by gas lamps, and every dining table was laid, just in case any of the members wished to use them. There were framed photographs on all the walls, a gallery of rich male Darksiders laughing and joking and sneering. Of Edwin Rafferty, however, there was no sign.

Frustrated, Jonathan threw himself down on a sofa in a lavish library, where cavernous bookshelves were crammed with leather volumes. Looking up, he saw something that chilled him to the bone. Directly in front of him was a life-size portrait of Vendetta. The banker was dressed in a white linen suit smeared with bloodstains. A body was slumped by his feet. It felt as if the vampire's eyes were burning deep into Jonathan's soul. He had hoped that he would never have to see that face again.

Jonathan rose to his feet and slowly approached the painting. He reached out and touched it, flinching in case it should bite back. By the side of the painting was a small plaque that read G. VENDETTA, WHOSE GENEROUS DONATIONS FROM HIS PRIVATE LIBRARY FILL THESE BOOKSHELVES. Jonathan shuddered. It was impossible to imagine Vendetta doing anything generous or kind.

He moved away from the painting and wandered around the room, running a finger across the gnarled spines of the books. All of the volumes appeared to be nonfiction: historical studies of feuds and wars, economic guides to financial scams and cons, and biographies of famous Darkside criminals. Portraits of exotic characters such as Charlie Redblood, Morticia della Rosa, and Solomon Razzaq glowered up at him.

Eventually Jonathan's finger came to rest on a large, bound volume with a midnight blue spine. He pulled it from the shelf and read the title: *Regretts' Darkside Peerage.* Its pages were filled with hundreds of biographies of well-to-do Darkside families. On a whim, Jonathan leafed through the pages until he came to the letter "R." He was faintly surprised to find an entry for the Rafferty family:

Rafferty, Ralph

The Rafferty family can boast of one of the most distinguished linages in Darkside. Ralph Rafferty (d. DY62) was an Irish seaman who was one of the first criminals to be sent to Darkside. Using his Lightside links, Ralph constructed a smuggling empire at Devil's

Wharf— which at that stage consisted only of a small jetty and two warehouses. His business acumen was such that, by DY45, it was estimated that over half of the products arriving from Lightside were transported by Rafferty's ships. Unsurprisingly, such success attracted the attentions of the Ripper, and Ralph was quick to place his smuggling network at Jack's disposal. Ralph's endeavors ensured that his family has enjoyed close ties to Darkside's first family ever since. Upon his death, Ralph was succeeded by his son, Lionel, with Lionel's art-enthusiast son, Edwin, the heir apparent to the family business. . . .

There was a crash and a loud cry from the room next door, startling Jonathan into dropping the book. His natural instinct was to stay in the safety of the library, but the voice sounded familiar. Gathering himself, Jonathan raced out of the library through the connecting door, and straight into pandemonium.

10

Amidst a casual air of luxury, the aroma of velvet and wood polish, and the silver gleam of burnished candlesticks, two men were tearing each other to pieces by the fireplace. A heavy poker had smeared soot on the red carpet near them, tantalizingly out of reach. One of the men was dressed all in black, and had a purple handkerchief wrapped around his face. He had gained the upper hand in the scuffle, and was pinning down the other man — the editor of *The Darkside Informer*, Lucien Fox.

Lucien was straining every sinew to hold off his attacker, but his frail physique was no match for his taller, fitter opponent. With a snarl, the man broke free from the editor's grip and punched him in the temple. Lucien slumped backward onto the carpet in a daze.

"Hey!" Jonathan cried out, and ran toward them.

The assailant whirled around, poised to spring at this new figure. Suddenly aware of the danger he was in, Jonathan took a step backward. Then a door crashed open on the other side of the room and Carnegie barreled in, hat askew. He grinned wolfishly at Lucien's attacker.

"I can't believe you started without me! Tell you what. You finish off the boy, and then me and you'll play together. Does that sound fair?"

The man's eyes narrowed, sizing up the detective. As Carnegie flexed his claws he made up his mind, and raced back toward the window. Before anyone could stop him, the attacker had wrenched up the window and jumped up onto the sill. Then, with a final flourishing salute, he was gone. Jonathan and Carnegie ran over to the window and watched him scamper away over the rooftops of the surrounding buildings.

"Not bad," Carnegie said, a note of approval in his voice. "We seem to be running into a better class of goon these days." He turned to Jonathan. "And what were you planning to do back there? Kick him in the shins?"

"I hadn't thought that far ahead. I was pleased to see you, though."

A noise came from behind them.

"Don't worry about me. I'm fine."

Lucien was rubbing his head vigorously, and mumbling oaths under his breath. Jonathan went over and helped him into a chair. A series of coughs scraped the editor's chest, and he dabbed a trickle of blood away from his mouth with a handkerchief. Lucien looked up, and noted Jonathan's look of concern with a rueful smile.

"Tell me, young Starling, does *everyone* who works with you get hit over the head?"

"Generally it's just the boy," Carnegie replied. "What happened?"

"I'm not entirely sure. I was poking around this floor for clues, when suddenly that guy jumped out from the shadows and tried to brain me with that thing." Lucien nodded at the poker, wincing with the pain the sudden movement caused. "Given the size of him, I was lucky he missed."

A thought occurred to Jonathan. He turned to the were-man. "Do you think it was that guy from the Midnight?"

"Correlli? Hardly. He doesn't hide his face. He likes people to know who they're dealing with. No, this was a different person trying to kill us." The wereman cocked his head. "But what was he doing hiding in here?"

Scratching his head, Carnegie moved across the room in search of clues. As the wereman began tapping the walls for secret doors, Jonathan noticed that there was a gap in the series of photographs that dotted the wall near the fireplace. Moving an armchair out of the way, he saw the broken shards of a picture frame strewn across the carpet.

"Hey, look at this!" Jonathan held up a piece of glass and showed it to Carnegie. "Looks like that guy was trying to get rid of some evidence."

Dropping down onto his hands and knees, Carnegie peered into the fireplace. Whatever had been thrown on the flames had long since burned down to ash, save for a scrap of singed newspaper that had fluttered away to the side of the hearth. The wereman snatched it up and glanced over it.

"Perhaps this wasn't a waste of time after all. Now, let's get out of here. Where's Arthur?"

As if in reply, there was a cry of pain from downstairs.

Lucien frowned. "That sounds like him. I presume the doormen have woken up."

Sighing, Carnegie pushed his hat back onto his head, muttered the word *journalists* as if it were a swearword, and marched purposefully out of the room.

It was sometime after three in the morning, and the offices of *The Informer* were quiet. The latest edition had been finished and placed in the eager hands of the young street hawkers. The rusty beasts of printing presses that spent the days growling in the basement slumbered now. Most of the journalists had left the building in search of new stories or other, darker distractions, leaving only a small circle of people grouped around a desk in the editor's office. Their shapes cast long shadows in the candlelight.

"I guess it's a lead," Arthur was saying, "but what now?"

The reporter's eye was swollen shut. Carnegie had made it down to the ground floor just in time to save him from receiving further punishment from the doormen. Their exit from the Cain Club had been hasty, and accompanied by screamed threats and thrown chairs. After the bedlam of the last couple of hours, the dim quiet of *The Informer* offices came as a welcome relief for Jonathan. He stifled a yawn. He felt as though he hadn't slept for a month.

Trying to stay alert, he leaned in over the table and read the clipping again. Within the blackened edges of the paper it was just possible to discern the following words:

The cream of Darkside society was present for the masked ball at the Cain Club celebrating the anniversary of Thomas Ripper's accession to the throne. Among those present were five eligible young men calling themselves "The Gentlemen." (See photo above. From left to right: Brother Heart, Brother Rake, Brother Spine, Brother Steel, and Brother Fleet.)

Without the accompanying photograph, it didn't tell them much. Jonathan tried to think positively.

"Well . . . we know Brother Spine was Edwin, and we've heard of Brother Fleet before. At least we know the names of the rest of the Gentlemen now."

"Which is all well and good," Arthur replied. "It would be nice if we could see their faces, though. I'm guessing that's why our mystery man set fire to it."

Lucien scratched his beard. "It's not all bad news, you know. The clipping looks like one of ours, after all — something from the society pages. I'll get someone to go back over the archives and try and find when it's from. Then we could get our hands on the original photograph."

Arthur sighed. "Have you seen the state of our archives recently? That could take years. If only Theresa were here."

"Why do you say that?" asked Jonathan.

"She used to cover the society stuff." He fingered the scrap of paper thoughtfully. "This could even have been one of her pieces."

Immediately Jonathan was wide awake, wild thoughts racing through his mind. His mom had known about the Gentlemen. Was it possible that she was connected to this mystery? He was about to speak when a creaking sound stole up from the main offices below. Carnegie shot a questioning look at Lucien, who shook his head.

"Everyone's gone," he said. "There shouldn't be anyone down there."

The wereman got up from his chair and opened the door an inch. He peered down the staircase.

"There is now," he reported. "Let's go and see what they're up to."

He headed out onto the staircase, his feet padding softly on each step. Behind him, Jonathan marveled at how such a huge creature could move so stealthily. He wondered how many Darkside villains had lived to rue that fact.

The candles had burned low in the main office, and it was only possible to make out the shapes and outlines of desks, coat stands, and drawing boards. Someone was rifling through the drawers of the desk in the far corner of the room. With a jolt, Jonathan realized that was where his mom had worked. A spar of anger stabbed him in the chest.

"Hey, you!"

The figure spun around to see Carnegie throw himself forward, cutting off his escape route. He could only stand there as the others came closer. Lucien held up a candle and swore, his shoulders slumping with relief.

"Harry! What on Darkside are you doing here?"

The reporter was quick to regain his composure.

"Hello there, boss. Didn't realize that anyone was still in the office."

"What are you doing going through my mom's stuff?" Jonathan demanded.

Harry airily adjusted his cuffs. "All that talk of the Ripper murder got me thinking. I was going to write a follow-up piece on how no one's come close to finding out who did it. Arthur told me once that Theresa spent a lot of time covering events at the Cain Club — I thought I'd see if she'd written anything about James Arkel." He looked squarely at Jonathan, a flicker of amusement in his eyes. "No need to get all excited."

"That's her private stuff! You shouldn't be going through it."

Rage boiled away inside Jonathan. At that moment the urge to hurt Harry, to wipe the smug smile from his face, was overwhelming. He squared up to the larger boy, who looked down with unfeigned amusement. Eventually Jonathan felt a heavy hand on his shoulder, pulling him away.

"Enough of that, boy. You've been spending too much time in Darkside for your own good." Carnegie eyeballed Harry. "And you're as stupid as you are cocky. I get nervous when people start creeping around in the dark. I tend to eat first and ask questions later. You under-stand me?"

Harry nodded.

The wereman gestured at the door. "Good. Now get out of here. And leave the Ripper murder alone!"

When he had left, Lucien shook his head. "That kid is more trouble than he's worth. I might fire him anyway."

Jonathan sat himself down in his mom's chair and began tidying up the mess, handling notebooks and clippings as if they were ancient relics. His hand settled on a newspaper in her top drawer that boasted bold headlines and pictures of beautiful celebrities. It was an old edition of a Lightside newspaper — and compared to the grim, dense print of *The Informer*, it was a carnival of color. He held it up.

"Check it out! It's a newspaper from my part of town."

Arthur and Lucien exchanged arch glances.

"I'm surprised Theresa wasted her time reading that sort of rag," the editor said stiffly. "Vacuous nonsense."

Arthur reached a pudgy hand over and began flicking through the newspaper.

"You mind if I borrow this? It's a fairly good example of how *not* to write a headline."

"Be my guest."

Jonathan drummed his fingers on the table, thinking. It felt as though pieces of the puzzle were floating around inside his head — if only he could fit them all together.

"When was James Arkel murdered again?" he asked slowly.

"I told you," Carnegie replied. "Twelve years ago: twenty-fourth of January, DarkYear 106."

"That's the same year my mom disappeared, isn't it?"

The wereman nodded. "Theresa vanished a couple of months afterward."

And with that, two puzzle pieces slotted neatly into place. Jonathan leapt up and waved the singed clipping in Carnegie's face.

"Don't you see? James's murder and my mom's disappearance are connected. This article proves it! She must have found out that the Gentlemen had something to do with the murder. They must have tried to silence her!"

Jonathan stopped short, his stomach suddenly lurching. If Theresa had discovered the Gentlemen's secret, what would they have done to keep her quiet? Both James Arkel and Edwin Rafferty were dead, murdered in the most dramatic and visible way. But no sign of Theresa had ever been found. She had just . . . vanished.

Arthur laid a hand on his arm. "Listen, Jonathan," he said softly. "It's only natural you want to find out what happened to your mom. But this scrap of paper doesn't prove anything. If Theresa did somehow find out who killed James, why didn't she tell anyone about it? Why didn't she speak to me or Lucien? It's the first rule of investigative journalism, son: Don't try to make the facts fit your theory."

"I can't explain it — it just makes sense! It's like one of your hunches, Arthurz. I know I'm right." He looked at Carnegie. "Did my dad ever say anything to you about this?"

"Boy, I haven't seen Alain since your mother vanished. I don't know where he lives in your London, and if he's visited Darkside, he hasn't seen me."

A shiver of excitement ran down Jonathan's spine.

"That settles it, then. Time to go back to Lightside."

11

Carnegie was stretched out on the sofa in his office, gnawing merrily on a meaty joint of indeterminate origin. The sound of his teeth grinding through muscle and fat filled the room. From time to time he growled with contentment. When Jonathan entered from a side room, the wereman eyed him with undisguised amusement.

"Feel better now that you've changed?"

Jonathan looked down at himself and shrugged. He had become so used to wearing shirts and waistcoats that his old Lightside clothes felt strange on him, like a school uniform. Ever since he had made it over to Darkside, he had become less and less sure what *normal* actually meant.

"I don't know about *better*," he replied. "But I've changed. You sure you're not going to come with me?"

Carnegie shook his head, and tossed the joint out of the window.

"Lightside isn't my kind of place. There's plenty of things I can do here while you're away. Besides, you haven't seen your father for a while. It's right that you spend some time with him without me hanging around in the background." He glanced out of the window, gauging the time by the light outside. "We'd better get a cab. Your appearance might draw attention on the Grand, and that's never a good thing."

"Where are we going?"

"To a crossing point I've used a few times. It'll take us a while to get there, but it's the safest way."

"Boring," said Jonathan in a singsong voice.

"I don't know about you, but I could do with a bit of boring every now and again."

"Spoilsport."

The wereman paused, and then gave him a cryptic look.

"Yes," he said. "You have changed, all right."

The hansom cab rattled up steep, cobbled streets and down beneath wrought-iron railway bridges, and on through the shadows cast by rows of large factories. Gazing out of the carriage window, Jonathan was dizzied by the sheer scale of the borough; roads that intersected and spiraled around one another in fiendishly complicated knots, the rabbles of people who seemed to congregate on every street corner. He had no idea that Darkside was so huge. It was almost as if it were alive: a grimy, infested organism filling its lungs with smoke.

Finally, the cab clip-clopped into a quiet square. Small bric-a-brac shops dozed in the afternoon sun. In the center of the square, wealthy ladies walked arm in arm around a small, railed-off park. The atmosphere was calm, refined even.

"This is a bit different," Jonathan said.

Carnegie grimaced. "This is Lone Square. We're on the very edge of Darkside. Some of the people here like to put on airs, pretend they're from a different part of town. At heart, though, they're the same as the rest of us. Thieves and murderers to the last man and woman."

At a signal from Carnegie, the cab was brought to a faltering halt outside Rookwood Maps and Globes. Jonathan hopped out of the carriage and stared at the shop window while Carnegie haggled with the driver. An old, weather-beaten piece of parchment map was stretched across the window, showing a strange land that he had never seen before. The place-names and the directions were all in Spanish. Hearing the wereman coming up behind him, Jonathan pointed at the map.

"What's this?"

Carnegie looked startled. "Thought you'd recognize it. Haven't you ever heard of America?"

Jonathan looked again at the unfamiliar landmass. The map must have been centuries old. It didn't resemble the continent he knew. He thought about saying something, but then decided against it.

Inside, the shop was cramped and dingy. Giant cobwebs hung between ancient navigational instruments: compasses and sextants, even a ship's steering wheel. Globes squeaked as they spun gently in the breeze. Everywhere Jonathan looked there were maps hanging down from the ceiling, like bedsheets on a wash line. He was surprised by the fact that most of them claimed to show countries and continents on Lightside, slightly less by the fact that none of them bore the faintest resemblance to reality. Some were ancient, inaccurate sketches, while others — such as a star-shaped China — were completely made up.

One particularly ornate and unusual map caught Jonathan's eye: a whirling labyrinth of black streaks. With a start, he realized he was looking at a map of Darkside itself.

An elderly, dark-haired woman was seated behind a counter in the far corner of the shop, humming quietly to herself. Her face brightened when she caught sight of the wereman.

"Elias! I haven't seen you for so long, my dear!"

Her voice was soft, with the hint of a foreign accent at its edges. Carnegie swept his hat off, and bowed with a grace that took Jonathan by surprise.

"My apologies, Carmen. I have been distracted by certain circumstances. Namely, this boy."

Carmen rose from her chair and inspected Jonathan.

"Judging by his clothing, I would say he is not from Darkside. Would the child be looking to return to the other London?"

"As ever, my dear, you are correct. Would it be possible for him to visit your cellar? It'll be a return journey."

"By all means. It will cost you two shillings, though."

"Two? That's some price increase."

Carmen spread out her arms in a gesture of helplessness.

"These are uncertain times. Everyone knows the Ripper is ill. Change is in the air. People are not so interested in maps and globes. I have to make a living somehow."

Carnegie rooted around in his pockets and eventually located two shining coins. Carmen accepted them quickly, and before Jonathan could blink they had been secreted in the folds of her dress. She gestured to Jonathan to follow her, and headed through a doorway covered with string beads. In the hallway beyond, she kicked a rug aside, revealing a trapdoor set into the floor. With a slight grunt of effort, Carmen hauled up the trapdoor and stepped to one side, making a flourishing gesture with her hands like a magician's assistant.

"Ta-da," she said, grinning.

Jonathan peered down. All he could make out was a flight of stone steps leading off into the blackness.

"That's it?"

Carmen lit a candle and handed it to him. "That's it. Just go down the steps, and along the passageway. There's not much more to it."

And with that, she headed back into the shop, the folds of her skirt bounding around her ankles like excitable puppies. Carnegie watched her go admiringly.

"Fine woman, Carmen. She's got less scruples than most of the thieves around here, though. Two shillings is robbery in all but name."

As the wereman griped, Jonathan suddenly realized that he was going to miss him. They had spent almost all of the last two months together. Jonathan had nearly been killed several times (more than once at Carnegie's own hands), but every day he had woken up and felt alive, felt the blood pumping through his veins in anticipation of what was to follow. Not only had the wereman saved his life, he had helped create an entirely new and vibrant existence for him.

Carnegie coughed uncomfortably, ending the prolonged silence.

"You even think about trying to hug me, you'll regret it, boy."

"Wasn't going to."

"Good . . . then, um . . . give my regards to your father. And don't get yourself killed."

He said the last sentence very quickly and then looked away, as if he was ashamed. Jonathan smiled.

"Yeah. You, too. I'll see you in a couple of days."

Cupping a hand around the candle to protect the flame,

he cautiously descended the steps, and slipped away into the darkness.

Jonathan had become so accustomed to nasty surprises that he was almost disappointed that the journey proved as simple as Carmen predicted: The steps led out onto a passageway that sloped gently upward for about a hundred yards before abruptly stopping at a door. As he approached the door, however, Jonathan could feel his chest tightening, and a sudden feeling of nausea in his stomach. His pulse started racing, and there was a searing pain in his temple. He knew there were nasty side effects to crossing. The festering atmosphere of Darkside was as much poison to strangers as it was oxygen to its inhabitants. Being half-Darksider, Jonathan was supposed to cope better than others, but even he was in pain. He thought back to his dad, crossing all those years ago, and wondered: *How much had it hurt him?*

Jonathan dropped to all fours and concentrated on taking slow, deep breaths. After a couple of minutes the pain subsided, although the nausea remained. He got back to his feet, and cautiously pushed the door open. It led out onto a dirty, deserted alleyway, where wooden crates and overflowing garbage cans slumped against the walls. Closing the door behind him, Jonathan saw that the alley was a dead end, and that the only exit led out onto a considerably busier road. Streams of people were walking to and fro: Lightsiders. He was back. Jonathan took a deep breath and walked up the alleyway and into the fading daylight, where he blinked with surprise. He was on Oxford Street.

Jonathan had lost count of the times he had wandered down this famous road when he was younger, jostling shoulder to shoulder with the crowds as they swarmed along the sidewalks and into the large department stores. Yet what had once been so mundane and familiar now seemed alien. The Darkside stench of sewers and horse dung was gone, and the air here felt crisp and metallic by comparison. Instead of horse-drawn carriages, a procession of red buses inched along the road, overwhelming Jonathan with the smell of exhaust and the chugging sound of engines. Almost everyone who walked by seemed to be talking into a cell phone, which they clasped precariously between their ear and their shoulder as they rearranged their shopping bags. Shop windows beamed with electronic displays and vibrant advertisements.

But it was more than just the technology. Whereas on

Darkside Jonathan felt menaced and threatened by every passerby, here no one gave him a second glance. He was just another kid. Couples pushed past him, smiling and chatting with each other, laden down with parcels and shopping bags. Looking up at the festive lights that had been strung out across the street, Jonathan realized that it was early December: People were Christmas shopping. Smiling Santas were everywhere. No wonder it was so busy.

Farther down Oxford Street, a section had been pedestrianized to afford shoppers more space. Jonathan joined them in the center of the road, marveling at the smoothness of the sidewalk. In eight weeks he had become accustomed to the feel of cobblestones beneath his feet. He walked slowly, like a tourist, trying to take in every little detail. Music was blasting from the shopfronts, not the scratchy gramophone records that Carnegie listened to in his lodgings, but the insistent thumping beats of dance music.

Up ahead of him, a circle had formed around a street entertainer introducing his act:

"Ladies and gentlemen. I should state at this stage that I can only attempt the following feat after years of tuition from the grand masters of this secret art." He paused. "So if it goes wrong, blame them."

There was a slightly nervous titter in response. Jonathan turned and looked as a jet of flame shot up over the heads of the shoppers and into the air. As the onlookers clapped and cheered, the crowd parted just enough for Jonathan to see the fire-eater.

It was Correlli. Even in the freezing cold, he was still only wearing an open red waistcoat, exposing his bronzed chest to the elements. Jonathan could see more of his appearance than he had been able to during their previous encounter. The fire-eater was older than he had thought. He possessed the thickset physique of a wrestler, but there were flecks of gray in his thin, wiry hair. What on earth was he doing here on Lightside? As Jonathan stood and gaped, their eyes met.

Correlli held his gaze for a second but didn't react. Then he doused his flaming brand in a bucket and addressed the audience once more.

"And now, ladies and gentlemen, if I could ask for a volunteer to help me perform my most dangerous stunt. Let me see . . . there's a likely lad, right at the back. How about you, sir?"

He smiled, and pointed his fire-stick straight at Jonathan's heart.

12

All at once, everyone was looking at him, smiling with encouragement. Jonathan felt rooted to the spot. A barrage of questions assailed him. What was Correlli doing here? Had he known that Jonathan was going to be on Lightside? Surely he wouldn't dare to hurt him in front of all these people? The fire-eater lit a brand meaningfully, illuminating the sweat glistening on his chest, and gave Jonathan a challenging stare.

Oh, he would dare, all right. He'd positively enjoy it.

"I think the young man's shy!" Correlli laughed. "Why don't we give him a round of applause to encourage him?"

As the audience began clapping and cheering, the noise jolted Jonathan into action. With that, he was gone. He sprinted away, knowing that Correlli would follow him, and so was unsurprised to hear the fire-eater cry, "Thief!" and begin pounding after him. Correlli was a trained and cunning killer, whose reputation was known and feared across Darkside. Jonathan was just a boy. It should have been over in seconds.

But the truth of it was, the fire-eater didn't stand a chance. Years of evading truant officers and policemen had honed Jonathan into a sleek, elusive street-runner. The sound of pursuit was a familiar one, calming even. It focused his mind. Jonathan ran smoothly, slipping past people rather than barging into them, trying to look like someone who was racing for a bus rather than a shoplifter. Automatically, he obeyed all the rules he had formed over the years: sprinting east toward Oxford Circus in the hope of losing Correlli in the crowds; running in zigzags rather than a straight line; staying well away from shops to avoid the attention of security guards.

At Oxford Circus he sliced his way through the packs of foreign tourists, turned north, and headed up Portland Place. Looking over his shoulder, he knew that he had lost Correlli, but he didn't stop running until he had passed through the gates of Regent's Park. He caught his breath by a bench, elation pulsing through his veins. It had been a while since he had been chased through London, and in a strange way, he had enjoyed it. Correlli could push a knife against his throat in the darkness of the Midnight, but this was Jonathan's part of town.

Shaking his tired muscles down, he could have been mistaken for one of the joggers that labored past him in the encroaching gloom. Jonathan knew he was going to have to walk home. There were no coins in his pocket, and he had no idea where his bus pass was. It wasn't a problem. It was nice to reacquaint himself with the city he had grown up in: the London of coffee shops, cell phones, and skateboards.

Night was drawing in by the time Jonathan reached his street. As he neared home, doubt flooded into his mind. Would his dad be pleased to see him? Since Alain's last darkening, there had been a glimmer of hope that he might finally be able to open up, be more like a normal dad. Jonathan couldn't bear the thought that his father had once again become the silent, brooding apparition that had haunted their house for years.

Light spilled out from behind drawn curtains in the Starling house. His hands shaking, Jonathan pressed the doorbell. He heard footsteps coming down the hallway, and then the door opened. For a split second Jonathan thought that there was no one there, but then he looked down and saw a tiny woman with long blonde hair staring at him.

Mrs. Elwood screamed.

"It's all right!" Jonathan said hastily. "It's me!"

She put her hand over her mouth in shock before crying joyfully, "Jonathan!" and wrapping her arms around his waist, squeezing him tightly. "It's so good to see you! Such a surprise!" she said. "We weren't sure if you were going to come back! ALAIN! JONATHAN'S HOME!"

Mrs. Elwood took Jonathan's hand and led him inside and into the kitchen. Although the house hadn't changed in his absence — the floorboards still creaked in the same places, and the air was still tinged with the musty odor of hundreds of old books — Jonathan felt strangely out of place, as if he were a guest in someone else's house. The electric light in the kitchen was too bright; the whirring of the dishwasher was an alien sound. As he looked around the room, Jonathan realized that Mrs. Elwood was talking to him.

". . . and I bet you must be starving. I'll fix something up for you right now. ALAIN! Where *is* that man? Probably got his head in a book." She paused. "Is everything all right? You look a bit spaced out."

"Yeah. I'm fine. It just feels a bit funny, being back in the house and all."

Mrs. Elwood nodded sympathetically. "Of course. You've been very far away, and . . . There you are!"

Jonathan turned around to see his dad standing in the doorway. Alain Starling was carrying a book in one hand and his glasses in the other, and had stopped in his tracks at the sight of his son. His hair was still prematurely gray, and his face etched with worry lines, but he seemed a little less drawn, a little less gaunt, than he had been in the past. They stood looking at each other for a couple of seconds before a broad grin broke out across Alain's face, and Jonathan knew everything was going to be all right.

He hadn't realized how hungry he was. Suddenly his plate was too small, and he couldn't pile enough food onto it. On the other side of the table, Alain and Mrs. Elwood studied Jonathan as he thrust his fork into a mountain of French fries.

"I'm glad that Elias is taking care of you," said his dad. "How is he these days?"

Jonathan thought for a second. "Short-tempered. Brutal. Rude."

"No change there, then." Alain laughed.

"It's odd. I can't really imagine you two as friends."

"Well, it was a long time ago. A lot's changed since then."

"I guess." Jonathan paused as he swallowed another mouthful and took a swig of Coke. "You look better, though. I wasn't sure . . . you know . . . how you were going to be."

"Oh, thanks." There was a note of surprised pride in his dad's voice. "I still have bad days every now and then, but I do feel better. I won't be running the London Marathon just yet, but you never know."

"Now that you're here, you are going to stay for a while, aren't you?" Mrs. Elwood cut in anxiously. "There's no need for you to go back *there*."

Jonathan put down his knife and fork. "I'm afraid not. I can only stay the night. I've come back for a reason."

A look of comprehension dawned on his dad's face. "Theresa?"

Jonathan nodded.

"I see. Finish your meal, and then we'll go and talk in my study."

After they had cleaned up the kitchen they went upstairs together, leaving Mrs. Elwood downstairs watching television. Jonathan was pleased to see that his dad's study — once little more than a prison cell — was unlocked, and the door open. The thick shutters that had prevented sunlight from entering the room had been taken down, and the stale atmosphere had lifted. Bathed in the soft light of a table lamp, it all seemed rather cozy.

Alain gestured at Jonathan to sit down in the chair, while he perched on the edge of the desk.

"So, then. What's going on, son?"

The story came out in a muddled rush, and several times Jonathan had to go back to explain parts again and insert crucial details. Alain listened intently, his eyes serious. When his son had finished, Alain thought for so long that Jonathan was almost worried he had reverted to his old catatonic self. Then he cleared his throat.

"I so badly wanted to go back to Darkside," he said, his voice husky. "In some ways, it drove me mad. Everything had been going so well. We were married; you'd just been born; and we'd finally decided to live permanently in the Darkside. Theresa was Darkside through and through, and crossing affected her badly. She couldn't spend more than a few days in Lightside without falling ill, whereas I could get by in Darkside. It wasn't always easy, but I had her, and you. And I know this might sound crazy to you, but we were happy there. Theresa loved her job at *The Informer*, and I had found some work in a watch shop. Darkside was so vibrant, so alive, that it made the rest of London look dreary. So we concocted a story that we were moving to South America, and went back to Lightside for one last time to tie up all the loose ends.

"We spent that morning — the last morning — doing normal things: shopping and the like. Then, over coffee, while we were sitting there reading the papers, Theresa suddenly went very quiet. Then she made some hurried excuse and went off on her own, without even finishing her food. That was the last time I saw her. Later that evening she left a message on the answering machine telling me she'd gone back to Darkside early. Maybe if I'd heard the phone I'd have been able to speak to her, persuade her to wait for me. But I was looking after you upstairs, and missed it.

"As soon as I listened to the message I should have gone back, but I didn't. After all, Theresa had lived in Darkside all her life: I knew she could look after herself. I still had a lot to sort out here, and — to be honest — I was angry at the way that she had run off. So it was a couple of days until I went back to the crossing point. But . . . there had been an accident. A building had caved in on top of the crossing point, burying it in tons of rubble. And that was that."

"Why didn't you go to another crossing point?" Jonathan burst out.

"Don't you understand? It was the only one I knew." The saddest of smiles touched Alain's lips. "I still wonder what the odds of that happening are. A thousand to one? A million to one? More? It was like I'd won some sort of horrible lottery. My prize was to lose my wife. To stay locked up in this room for over a decade, trying to find a way back to her."

Jonathan sat stupefied. It was the longest speech he'd ever heard his dad make. Twelve years later, it was still so raw for Alain. There were no tears in his eyes, just a deep emptiness in his soul. As he thought more about the story, a thought occurred to Jonathan.

"But if you were stuck here, how did you hear that Mom had gone missing in Darkside?"

A voice from behind Jonathan made him jump.

"Because I came here and told him."

Mrs. Elwood had slipped into the study unnoticed.

"WHAT? *You're* from Darkside?"

She nodded, biting her lower lip. Jonathan rubbed his face with disbelief. For years Mrs. Elwood had been the only constant in his life. He had depended on her so much. She had been so ordinary, so stable compared to everything else in his life. And now it turned out that — like everyone else — she wasn't the person Jonathan thought she had been.

"I am. I was a friend of your mother's. I saw her briefly when she came back from Lightside, and was one of the first to hear that she had vanished. I knew that someone had to tell Alain, so I raced over here to find him. I must have been one of the last people to make it through the crossing point before it collapsed."

"But surely you must have known another way to get back?"

Mrs. Elwood shook her head.

"You don't understand, Jonathan. Darksiders and Lightsiders don't mix. Most people don't cross back and forth like you do — the strain would kill them. The day I came over was the first time I had ever seen the rest of London. I used the one crossing point that most people knew about — it was quick and safe. When the building caved in on it, Alain wasn't the only person stranded here. Luckily for me, the crossing didn't affect me too badly, and I managed to adapt to Lightside. Before long I was even happy here, whereas your father, well . . ." She moved forward and patted Alain on the arm. "But you have to understand, I know just how evil Darkside is. That's why I don't want you to go back there. Either of you!"

Alain let out a long sigh. "The problem is, Jonathan has to go back."

"Why, in God's name?"

"Because I can't."

The words hung heavy in the air.

"The state I'm in now, just the atmosphere of that place would kill me. Unlike you, son, there's no Darkside in my blood. It's not easy for a Lightsider to live there. But you'll be all right. And if the murder of this Ripper really is linked to your mom's disappearance, you and Carnegie have to find out what's going on. You've got to continue the search for me." Alain swallowed hard, and when he spoke again, his voice cracked. "This . . . could be our only chance . . ."

In the silence that followed, Mrs. Elwood shook her head sadly and left the room. Jonathan let his father compose himself before turning to him.

"Dad? You know you said Mom left a message on the answering machine?"

Alain nodded.

"Have you still got it?"

A sad smile crossed his dad's face. Then, fishing a key from a chain around his neck, he opened up a box on his desk and pulled out a small cassette tape.

"I try not to put it on too much. Don't want it wearing out."

Alain slipped it into an antiquated machine and pressed PLAY. It beeped, and after a pause, a woman began speaking.

Her voice, tinged with an Irish accent, was agitated. Jonathan's dad closed his eyes.

"Alain? It's me. Look, I have to go back to Darkside early . . . tonight, in fact. I've found something out about a story I've been working on, and there's someone I urgently have to talk to. It can't wait. I didn't say anything because I knew you'd insist on coming with me, and I have to do this on my own. I'm sorry . . . but I'll see you in a couple of days, and everything will be all right again, I promise. I love you."

There was a click, and Theresa Starling was gone.

13

That night, tossing and turning in his old bed, his feet twitching underneath the covers, Jonathan was stalked through his dreams by a nightmarish creature that was part beast, part fire, and part shadow. He could hear the tramp of its feet as it hunted: slow and purposeful footfalls that never hurried, and never stopped. Jonathan wanted to run, but he felt as if his feet were trapped in mud. In his dream, places from his past merged seamlessly together. With agonizing slowness, he turned off the Grand and came out onto the playground from his old school. On the other side of the street was the greenhouse at Vendetta Heights. Jonathan stumbled past that until he reached the offices of *The Darkside Informer*, where the beast finally came to a halt. A wave of relief passed over Jonathan, until he looked back over his shoulder and saw why it had paused. Theresa was working at her old desk, her back to the beast. The beast growled softly, and padded toward her . . .

Jonathan woke up shouting and drenched in sweat. Later, reveling in the powerful jets of the shower, he resolved to go back to Darkside as soon as possible.

He said his good-byes that morning. The sky was grim and heavy with bulging clouds. Jonathan hugged his dad at the end of the driveway while Mrs. Elwood moped gloomily in the background.

"I'm sorry you have to go so soon," said Alain.

"Yeah. Me too. But I can't stop until I find out what's going on."

"At least let us take you back to the crossing point."

"Nah. I'll be fine. It's a long journey, and you need to build up your strength. And anyway," Jonathan added with a smile, "I don't want you getting all soppy on me in public."

Alain grinned. "Fair enough."

"Make sure you send word to us as often as you can," Mrs. Elwood called out. "We need to know you're OK!"

"I will. Try not worry. I've got Carnegie with me."

She made a face. "That's not much of a reassurance."

Alain hugged him again, and looked him straight in the eye. "I'm very proud of you," he said softly. "You know that, don't you, son?"

Jonathan nodded, a lump in his throat, and walked hurriedly away. He didn't look back as he continued down the street, scared that he might change his mind. There was a part of him that would have liked to have stayed in the house for a while — until Christmas, maybe even beyond that. Maybe he could have forgotten all about Darkside, with its gruesome inhabitants and ever-present danger. After all, Jonathan couldn't say for sure what he was going to do when he got back there. It was clear that his mom had seen something here that had sent her hurrying back to Darkside, but what? He had a gut feeling that it was connected to the Gentlemen and James Arkel's death, but there was no way of proving it.

However, as he headed down into the Underground and boarded a train, there was one thing Jonathan was sure about. He had heard his mom speak for the first time, a lilting voice colored with an Irish accent, and he had never felt closer to her. School and normality would have to wait. He *had* to find out what had happened to his mom.

*   *   *

Elias Carnegie could feel the animal rising within him.

It was late afternoon on Fitzwilliam Street. Tension reigned. Gusting winds whisked sheets of an old edition of *The Informer* into spirals high up in the air, while cobblestones echoed to the drumming of horses' hooves. The sun was dipping behind gap-toothed roofs and, as a parting gesture, slanted a weak ray of light across the wereman as he strode across the street, seemingly oblivious to the carriages that hurtled past him, missing him by inches.

Carnegie's senses had sharpened so much that he was in danger of being overwhelmed: the scent of horse dung smeared on a washerwoman's skirts; the sound of a coin being tapped absentmindedly against a lamppost far down the street; the outline of a weapon in a gentleman's jacket. But above all that, he was acutely aware of flesh and blood all around him. Carnegie had spent the day in his lodgings going back over the details of the Rafferty case, and had forgotten to eat. Now the raging animal inside him was hungry, and he had to satisfy it before it consumed him.

Every day was a battle between the two sides of his nature. Sometimes Carnegie felt so weary that he wanted to give in, and revel in the power and the simple pleasures of the beast. Life seemed so much easier when he changed form. There were no gray areas: just black and white — and red. He wondered whether Jonathan could ever understand how difficult it was for him. For all his fondness for the boy, there were times when Carnegie looked at him and saw merely fat, muscle, and bone. At those moments, Jonathan's life hung by a thread.

Dark thoughts. Carnegie moved swiftly into the butcher's shop and, with a curt gesture, caught the attention of the man behind the counter. Col's cheery greeting died in his throat. He gestured grimly at Carnegie to go through to the meat locker, then, after he had passed out of sight, tucked a large cleaver into his belt before turning to the next customer.

Though he was aware of his breath steaming in the cold environment of the freezer, Carnegie didn't register the change in temperature. He was focused on the slabs of meat that hung down from the ceiling. He cast an expert eye over them before selecting the closest to him. Suddenly the shabby private detective was gone, and a ravenous animal was ripping and tearing at the slab with sharp claws and teeth, gobbling down strips of meat without thought or feeling, barely even chewing. Dried flecks of blood stained his face and his hands.

It was as he was licking his fingers clean that Carnegie realized he wasn't alone. The cold had numbed his sense of smell, but he could just make out the sound of shallow breaths coming from somewhere in the room. The wereman grinned viciously.

"I'm not full yet," he called out. "I can always find room for warm flesh. Why you don't come out from your hiding place, whoever you are, and let's talk about it?"

On the other side of the room, Raquella stepped out from behind a meat rack. She was dressed in a black outfit — thick woolen overcoat, hat, scarf, and gloves — that stood out against the stark white backdrop of the freezer. The color had drained from her face: maybe from cold, maybe from fear. By contrast, blood was galloping through Carnegie's veins. Barely resisting the urge to lunge at the girl, the wereman slowly raised an eyebrow.

"A friendly face. That's a surprise."

"I'm sorry for disturbing you, Mr. Carnegie, but it was an urgent matter."

"So I can imagine. I must be getting predictable in my old age. I trust you haven't been waiting long for me?"

"An hour, maybe two. Not long."

Carnegie ran his tongue over his canines. Somewhere within his soul, a voice urged him to stay still, not to kill this one, to ask another question . . .

"How did you get in here?"

"I dodged past the butcher when he wasn't looking. It wasn't difficult."

"It might sound a bit old-fashioned, but you could have just come up to my lodgings."

She shook her head. "No one must know I've seen you. It's not just Vendetta — there are other considerations . . ."

Her voice was trembling, but she held herself together, standing upright and looking Carnegie right in the eye. *She works for Vendetta,* he reminded himself. *She has faced death before.* The wereman could feel his pulse rate starting to drop, and the first drops of compassion seep back into his bloodstream.

"You watched me eat?"

She nodded.

"My apologies. My table manners aren't the best."

Raquella smiled for the first time. "You needn't

apologize, Mr. Carnegie. I have a small brother. Believe me when I say I've seen worse."

Carnegie laughed huskily, and with a growl the beast inside him retreated back into a dark corner.

"Come on. We can't talk here. Let's think of a way to smuggle you back to my lodgings."

From his vantage point at the window of Carnegie's lodgings, Jonathan watched the wereman as he left the butcher's shop and crossed the street, carrying a huge hunk of meat wrapped in white cloth in his arms. The return journey from Lightside had been uneventful, but it had taken an age to get back to Fitzwilliam Street from Lone Square. As he moved through Darkside, Jonathan could feel the fetid atmosphere of the borough reclaiming him, sliding underneath his fingernails and nestling in his hair. He didn't want to admit it, but it wasn't an entirely unpleasant sensation.

He drew back from the window as he heard Carnegie stamping up the staircase. The wereman kicked his door open, struggling with the huge bundle of meat in his arms, and noted Jonathan's presence with equanimity.

"Oh. You're back. Close the curtains, boy."

Jonathan did as he was told, consigning the office to darkness. He went over to the wall and turned on a couple of gas lamps. As Carnegie gave up his struggle with his package and dropped it on the floor, Jonathan noted the flecks of blood dripping from his mouth, and the unfocused, bestial look in his eyes. There was a movement amid the streams of white cloth — a flailing black boot and a familiar shock of flaming red hair.

"Raquella! Are you OK?"

Jonathan glanced at Carnegie — was he eating his acquaintances now? The wereman noted his wide-eyed stare and snorted.

"Don't worry, boy. I'm full."

"I wasn't . . . it was just . . ." Jonathan guiltily scrabbled around for something to say.

"Don't help me up, then!"

Raquella fought her way out of the cloth and got to her feet, smoothing down her clothes in an attempt to regain her composure. She cast a baleful look at Carnegie before turning her attention to Jonathan.

"You're a real gentleman," she said tartly. "I thought you Lightsiders were meant to have manners?"

"I'm just surprised to see you, that's all. What are you doing here? Won't Vendetta kill you if he finds out?"

"He's still recovering. And, as you can see, we took precautions." She glanced sideways at Carnegie. "Though I find it hard to believe that was the best way."

The wereman shrugged. "You're here, aren't you? Now, why don't you tell us what's going on?"

Raquella sighed and sat down. She bowed her head for a few seconds, and when she looked up, Jonathan was shocked to see tears running down her cheek.

"It's my father," she said desperately. "He's gone missing. Or worse. I don't know. You've got to help me find him!"

14

Humphrey Granville sat back in his chair and licked his lips with anticipation. Tonight promised to be an unforgettable occasion. He had gone to great lengths in preparation, squeezing himself into an immaculately cut dinner jacket that bore the scars of battle with a thousand fine meals. He had dragged a comb through his hair and slicked it down with handfuls of grease. He had donned his finest bone cuff links — the left one in the shape of a knife, the right a fork. Only the crumbs in his mustache betrayed Humphrey's more disheveled day-to-day appearance.

The main dining room of The Last Supper, Darkside's most exclusive restaurant, hummed with contentment. Because there were only five tables in the restaurant — arranged in a pentagram — it was notoriously difficult to get a booking. Those diners fortunate enough to make a reservation kept silent about the fact for fear of having their identity stolen. Humphrey had been on the waiting list for five long years. He had been taking tea at the Savoy Hotel when word came through that he had finally got a table. It was all he could do to stop himself from doing a jig with glee. Immediately, Humphrey had set about organizing the trip back to Darkside.

He looked at the menu again. Choosing had not been easy, and it was impossible not to have second thoughts. Perhaps the seared raven might have been a better choice, or the renowned weasel risotto. Gaston La Guerre, the head chef of The Last Supper, was a foul-tempered ogre of a man, whose short fuse was matched only by his culinary perfectionism. There were many tales of unfortunate kitchen hands whose mistakes had led to their fingernails garnishing the soup of the day. Humphrey hoped that Gaston was in particularly fine form that evening.

Although everything should have been perfect, Humphrey had to admit that he was feeling troubled. The whole business with Nicholas was getting under his skin. He should never have listened to him. The problem was, ever since the Gentlemen had first come together in the

Cain Club, Humphrey had desperately sought Nicholas de Quincy's approval. Though they moved in the same refined circles, the Granvilles were gatecrashers who had stumbled into money through the deeply unglamorous business of pawnbroking. The aristocratic de Quincy — heir to a long-established blackmail fortune — never managed to disguise his contempt for Humphrey. He sneered constantly about his weight, his low connections, and his rudimentary manners. Humphrey was a jovial man, but in his darker moments even he had considered trying to bump Nicholas off.

After the murder of James Arkel, and the discovery that he was a Ripper, Darkside descended into anarchy. The Bow Street Runners, Thomas Ripper's feared henchmen, stalked the streets, arresting anyone who crossed their path. Panicking, the Gentlemen had fled their separate ways. While Humphrey raced over to Lightside, Edwin descended down the steps of the Midnight. Brother Steel — the one Gentleman Humphrey could genuinely say he liked, and the one Gentleman who had refused to take part in the plot — was ostracized by the rest of the group. Humphrey had neither seen nor heard from him again.

Only Nicholas — Brother Heart — had kept calm, and kept the counsel of Brother Fleet. It was he who found out that Fleet was James's brother, a Ripper also. And it was Nicholas who reappeared in Humphrey's life ten years later, with a typically underhanded blackmail plot. A de Quincy asking a Granville for assistance! Humphrey's chest swelled with pride as he accepted. However, as things turned out, it was a decision he had begun to regret even before Edwin was murdered.

Not that the same could happen to him — Humphrey had taken precautions. He checked over his shoulder, and was reassured to see the gigantic form of Jol standing impassively in the shadows. Jol was the most expensive bodyguard in Darkside, and was renowned for never letting one of his clients come to harm. Humphrey snorted. These were dangerous times, but Humphrey Granville knew what he was doing. There was no way that he was going to let anyone ruin his life, or stop him from enjoying his meal.

When the first course arrived, he knew that he wasn't going to be disappointed. The shark pâté smelled divine, and tasted even better. As he let it settle on his tongue, Humphrey detected a sharp flavoring that even he — the greatest gourmand in Darkside — couldn't identify. Gaston was indeed a master of his craft. He took a sip of wine and lingered over each mouthful.

The next two hours drifted languidly by in a glorious procession of tastes and sensations. Humphrey almost felt he was dreaming. He forgot all about Edwin and Jol, his attention consumed by the dishes that passed in front of him. The waiters were shadows that flitted in and out of the lights, clearing away dishes before the diners had even noticed them. With the arrival of each course came titters of excitement and gasps of surprise from the four tables around Humphrey. They chattered ceaselessly. Humphrey could never understand why anyone would want to disturb the enjoyment of their food by having company: He preferred to dine alone.

The sixth course was delivered with the lights turned low, to highlight the spectacle of the flambéed jellyfish. As he stared into the flickering flames, Humphrey reluctantly admitted that all this rich food was taking its toll. He was beginning to feel woozy. Beads of sweat were forming on his brow. Perhaps eating a second hyena steak had been a bad idea. Humphrey steeled himself and took a large gulp of water. This was ridiculous! The meal of a lifetime, and he was flagging by the sixth course! He picked up his knife, and attacked the jellyfish with renewed gusto.

His reverie was interrupted by a chilling scream from the kitchen. Humphrey looked up fearfully at Jol. The hulking bodyguard lumbered forward to investigate, crashing through the swing doors that led into the kitchen. Humphrey's earlier mood of defiance was ebbing away, unease growing like his feeling of indigestion. For all his bullishness, the fact remained that Edwin had been brutally murdered in an alleyway, and there was no way of knowing whether that would be the end of the matter. Though they had known Brother Fleet for years, he was still a Ripper, and therefore capable of anything. Humphrey dabbed at his face with a napkin. The floor felt like it was tilting, as the tables revolved around him like some sort of carnival ride.

Jol returned from the kitchen with a blank expression on his face.

"What's going on in there?" asked Humphrey nervously.

"Turned out one of the golden eagles they're going to fry wasn't as dead as everyone thought it was. It attacked one of the sous chefs."

"Is everything all right now?"

"I guess so. They're both dead." Jol passed a critical eye over his client. "You OK? You don't look so good."

"Yes, yes. I'll be fine. Just make sure there's no one watching me."

"How's the food?"

Humphrey glared at him irritably. "You'll never know. Now go away and leave me in peace."

As Jol retreated Humphrey placed his head in his hands. The bodyguard was right — he was feeling unwell and increasingly rattled. There was no need to snap at his only protection. The room was beginning to spin faster and faster, making him feel disoriented. His stomach was bubbling furiously, and the sharp flavor he had detected in the shark pâté had reclaimed his mouth.

"Jol?" he groaned.

The bodyguard was by Humphrey's side in a flash. "What's up?"

"I don't feel well." He groaned again, clutching his stomach. "I think someone might have put something in the food."

"Right. Let's get out of here."

Jol wrapped an arm around the portly man, hauled him to his feet, and led him toward the swing doors at the back of the restaurant.

"Where are we going?" asked Humphrey weakly.

"Too many people out front. We're leaving through the service exit."

The bodyguard maneuvered the pair of them through the doors and into the kitchen of The Last Supper. The room was in a state of bedlam. Chefs in long, greasy aprons ran up and down the narrow gangways, shouting and threatening one another with kitchen knives. Rows of ovens churned out heat like a blacksmith's forge. Clouds of steam billowed from pots rattling on the oven tops, while jets of flame shot from blackened frying pans. In the chaos, no one seemed to notice the interlopers.

Jol pushed Humphrey on through the kitchen, and into the cavernous pantry at the back of the building. The size of a small barn, the gloomy pantry was home to stock-piles of raw ingredients and tethered wild animals. The floor was splattered with grain and rotten vegetables. Glancing around to make sure the area was safe, Jol sat Humphrey down on a sack of potatoes.

"Sit tight. Going back in to check something."

"Don't leave me!" Humphrey quivered, but it was too late. Jol had slipped away, closing the door behind him. Humphrey shivered violently. The drafty pantry was worse than the boiling kitchen. He was definitely coming down with some sort of fever. Sweat was running down his face in rivulets.

There was a rustling sound from behind a grain mountain.

"Hello?" Humphrey called out. "Who's there?"

There was a cawing sound in reply. He relaxed a little. Just one of the birds. It must have been one of the exotic items on the menu, for he didn't recognize the sound of its call.

The bird cawed again, more insistently this time. The thought occurred to Humphrey that, if someone was after him, the noise might attract their attention.

"Shh!" he hissed. "Nice birdie! Shhh!"

The bird cawed again, as if it were playing some sort of game.

"If you don't shut up I'll eat you raw!"

A piercing shriek filled the pantry, battering Humphrey's eardrums. There was the sound of flapping wings, and then to his horror he saw a wave of darkness rolling through the air toward him. Frozen with fear, Humphrey barely had time to shield himself before the cloud enveloped him. The smell of rotting meat filled his nostrils, and he felt a slicing pain down the side of his face. Humphrey fell to his knees, blood streaming down his cheek. From somewhere within the cloud, the creature shrieked again, in triumph this time.

Overcome with panic, Humphrey looked up to see the black shape swooping up into the rafters, banking around to come at him again. He staggered to the pantry door and turned the handle. It was locked. He rattled the door violently, screaming at the top of his lungs, but no one came running to help him, and he was too weak to break it down. Humphrey slumped sobbing onto the floor, defenseless in the face of whatever nightmare was hidden in the darkness. The last thing that ran through his mind before the creature descended on him was: Where had his bodyguard gone?

Jol turned the key in the lock, and walked away from the pantry door. He had no intention of listening to the carnage. It was enough to put a man off his dinner. He returned to Granville's table and settled back in the chair, which creaked as it struggled to deal with the bodyguard's vast weight. In an unlikely display of refinement, he unfolded a napkin and tucked it into his collar.

A waiter emerged from out of the kitchen and swept up to the table.

"Has sir's companion left?" he asked politely.

"I'm afraid so," Jol replied. "And he won't be returning. How many courses are left?"

"Still seven to go."

"Good. How's the food?"

The waiter smiled. "Haven't you heard, sir? They say it's good enough to die for."

15

The carriage was silent. Watching Raquella as she anxiously chewed on a fingernail, Jonathan wanted to say something to reassure her and comfort her, but he couldn't think of anything. In a strange way he had been lucky — his mom had disappeared so long ago that it didn't feel like he had lost her, because he couldn't remember Theresa being there in the first place. How much worse must it be to lose someone you had known and loved for years?

Though his sympathy for Raquella was heartfelt, it couldn't quite stem the rising tide of excitement within Jonathan. He was certain that Theresa had discovered something about the Gentlemen that had tied them to James Ripper's murder. Maybe they had kidnapped her. It wasn't as if they *had* to kill her, Jonathan told himself firmly. Maybe she was imprisoned in a building nearby, waiting for someone to come and rescue her. Maybe he passed by her every day. He knew one thing for sure: One of the Gentlemen had to know what had happened to Theresa. If they could solve James Ripper's murder, would it lead them to his mom? The prospect was almost too enormous to entertain.

Alongside Jonathan, Arthur Blake stared thoughtfully out of the window. The portly reporter had bustled into Carnegie's office in a state of breathless excitement. Completely ignoring Raquella, he had launched into a speech.

"There's been another murder!" he panted. "Just like the Rafferty one. I was interviewing a ghoul with the Pierce boy down on Nowhere Street when I got the tip. A guy has been butchered inside The Last Supper. I managed to slip in around the back and see the body before it was taken away. Judging by the state of it, whoever killed James and Edwin killed this guy as well."

Even Jonathan had heard of The Last Supper, and had walked past the heavily guarded entrance on several occasions. It seemed strange to imagine someone losing their life inside.

"What was his name?" he asked.

"The restaurant was trying to hush it up, but I slipped the maître d' a couple of shillings and he told me it was a guy called Humphrey Granville." He looked at the wereman keenly. "Mean anything to you?"

Carnegie shook his head.

"Me neither. But it's a new lead, and someone's got to know who he is. Let's go!"

He made for the door, only to be stopped in his tracks as a hairy hand landed on his shoulder. Carnegie twisted Arthur around so they were facing each other.

"As exciting as this news is, you appear to have left your manners back at the restaurant. The young lady you've been ignoring is Raquella Joubert. She is a friend of ours."

Arthur nodded a bewildered greeting at the maidservant. "Oh . . . h-hello there, miss. I didn't see you there."

Carnegie pulled the reporter up to him so their faces were almost touching.

"Raquella's father has gone missing. Naturally, she's very upset, and we're going to see what we can do to help her. Then, maybe, we'll go and investigate this Granville fellow."

"O-of course," Arthur stammered, his feet scrabbling for purchase on the ground. "She is a f-friend, after all."

The wereman grinned, and let the reporter drop to the floor. "Glad we cleared that up. Shall we go, then?"

And now they were pulling up outside a modest, terraced house in the Lower Fleet. Farther up the street, children were scampering across the cobblestones and playing on the sidewalk, but there was no one outside this house. Raquella climbed slowly out of the carriage and led them to the front door.

Jonathan felt more nervous about entering the Joubert house than he had in almost any other place in Darkside. He felt like an intruder, especially with Carnegie and Arthur clumping alongside him. There was a mournful atmosphere in the hallway, echoes of private grief. A low murmur of voices was coming from the downstairs front room. Jonathan followed Raquella through the door, and gasped.

It was dark in the small room, and the faint sound of children's laughter drifted in from the street through the drawn curtains. Georgina Joubert was sitting on the sofa, cradling a small baby in her arms. Her drawn face spoke of a tearful, sleepless night. And next to her, calmly pouring out a cup of tea from the pot, was Marianne.

Instinctively, Jonathan tensed. The bounty hunter was dressed sympathetically in black, and her hair was an identical shade of burnished raven. The last time Jonathan had seen her was when she had dived into The Beastilia Exotica's Pool of Pain to rescue her henchman, Humble. He still remembered her white hair flashing in the lights. Though he should have hated Marianne — she was dangerous, and she had put both his and Alain's life in mortal danger — Jonathan had to admit on seeing her that his feelings were slightly more complex than that.

She looked up as they entered, and smiled.

"Hello, everyone. How are we all?"

A low growl rumbled from Carnegie's throat. Marianne kept on talking as she filled a second cup.

"There's not enough tea for you all, I'm afraid. You should have told Georgina you were coming."

"Marianne," said the wereman, through clenched teeth. "I'm surprised to see you here."

"I just thought I'd come around and see how the Jouberts were doing. This business puts such a terrible strain on a family, you know."

"She's been ever so kind," Georgina whispered. "Please, won't you all sit down?"

They arranged themselves uncomfortably on an assortment of chairs. Jonathan could see that Carnegie was inwardly seething. The weremen flexed his fingers, as if he were itching to throttle Marianne, and sent a volley of vicious glances in the bounty hunter's direction. If Georgina was aware of the threat of violence in the air, she chose to ignore it. She handed Raquella the baby and took a cautious sip of her tea.

"It's very good of you to come, Mr. Carnegie, but I'm not sure what you could do to help us. My William's vanished into thin air, and I don't know why."

"Raquella said that there was a note mentioning some kind of secret."

A shadow passed across Georgina's face.

"Whatever it was, he kept it well hidden from me. Oh, don't get me wrong, I knew that *something* had happened. We didn't always live like this." She gestured at the cramped sitting room. "During the first years of our marriage, William had real prospects. He had a job lined up in the most lucrative bank in Darkside. He was going to be one of the most important men in the borough, and everyone knew it. The jealous looks I used to get when we went out riding in our carriage . . ."

Georgina smiled at the memory, then looked down at her cup. When she spoke again, her voice was brittle.

"And then we received a letter from the bank informing us that the job offer had been withdrawn. Just like that . . . it was gone. Something in William died that day. He tried to get other work, but everywhere he went doors were slammed in his face. It was as if someone was trying to stop him from getting any sort of job. And it wasn't just work, either. All our friends turned their backs on us. No one would help. William couldn't even get into the Cain Club anymore."

Jonathan and Arthur exchanged wide-eyed glances. The reporter was about to ask a question when suddenly the door to the front room opened and Humble and Skeet entered.

Thinking about it, Jonathan should have known that Marianne wouldn't have come here alone. Even so, it was a shock to be suddenly confronted with them. The giant mute Humble's head brushed the ceiling of the room, forcing him to hunch over. His face was lined with jagged scars, a reminder of his brush with death in the Pool of Pain. Incongruously, a small child was clinging to his trouser leg. At the sight of Jonathan, his ever-present smile faltered, and malice glinted in his eyes. The feral Skeet followed closely behind, his bald head twitching with nervous energy. Both creatures were dressed in their usual undertakers' outfits, which seemed horribly appropriate given the funereal air of the Joubert house.

Instinctively, Carnegie sprang to his feet, claws at the ready. He would have charged forward had Jonathan not held his arm and gestured at Georgina, who was taking her baby back from Raquella. The wereman glared at the boy, but then sat back down. At the same time, Marianne looked over at Humble and shook her head.

"It's always nice when old friends meet," she said cheerfully. "But let's catch up at a more . . . *appropriate* time, shall we?"

Behind Georgina's back, Humble made a throat-slitting gesture at Jonathan. Skeet uttered a small, impatient sound, his hands straying behind his back, where, Jonathan presumed, he had stored a weapon.

"Danny's not being a nuisance, is he?" Georgina absently asked the mute.

Humble shook his head, the grin returning to his face. He patted the small boy on the head.

"Humble gets on famously with children," Marianne said proudly. "They love him."

Arthur cleared his throat. "I'm sorry to press you, Mrs. Joubert, but you mentioned something about the Cain Club earlier. William was a member there?"

"A member? He practically lived there — before he met me, of course. He was always spending time with those friends of his. A right gang of mischief makers they were, too."

Suddenly everything fell into place for Jonathan. "He was friends with Humphrey Granville, wasn't he?"

Georgina looked surprised. "I wasn't supposed to know, you understand. They were so secretive, wearing masks and calling one another 'Brother this' and 'Brother that.' But William told me about some of his friends — The Gentlemen, they called one another — and Humphrey was one of them. He was known as Brother Rake."

Everybody sat up. Even Humble looked interested. Jonathan's mind was racing. If Raquella's father was tied up in all of this, it was little wonder he had fled. But where to? The killer had managed to track down both Edwin and Humphrey. Was anywhere in Darkside safe? The atmosphere in the room, already tense, had been electrified by the revelation. Georgina kept on talking, dreamily oblivious.

"But when things turned sour for William and me, his 'friends' disappeared just like everyone else. It was a horrible time for him. For both of us."

Raquella squeezed her mother's arm, who gave her a sad smile in return.

"Still, I can't complain," Georgina said, trying to put a brave face on things. "I've got the children to look after me."

"Georgina," Carnegie said softly. "This could be important. Can you remember any more of William's friends?"

She frowned. "It was such a long time ago. There were five Gentlemen, thick as thieves they were . . . William, Humphrey, and . . . oh, *him*." Georgina shuddered. "An odious man, he was. Came around to our house a couple of times, didn't have a good word to say about anybody. De Quincy, he was called. Nicholas de Quincy. A blackmailer. Why? Do you think he might have something to do with William going missing?"

"I don't know for certain," Carnegie replied. "But we're going to make absolutely sure we find out. Do you know where this de Quincy lives now?"

Georgina shook her head. "I haven't seen the man in over a decade. And I'll be quite happy if I don't see him again for another."

Marianne finished the last of her tea and placed the saucer gracefully on the table. "Well, Georgina. I think we've imposed on you long enough."

Producing a pen and a piece of paper, she quickly wrote something down and folded it up. Then she kissed Raquella's mother on the cheek. "If you need anything, don't hesitate to get in touch."

She turned to the rest of the room.

"It's been lovely seeing you all again. Let's not leave it so long next time, shall we?"

Marianne dropped the piece of paper into a surprised Jonathan's lap, winked, and flowed out of the room. Humble gently disentangled Danny from his leg and followed her.

His hands trembling slightly, Jonathan unfolded the note and read Marianne's message.

"What is it?" asked Carnegie.

"Directions," Jonathan replied. "She's told us where we can find Nicholas de Quincy."

16

One o'clock in the morning, and three figures were standing next to a carriage pulled over by the side of a dirt track. They had traveled many miles southwest, away from the perpetual chaos of the Grand, over the haunted arches of Baelmonk Bridge, and out onto narrow, rutted tracks that ran past the sickly brown hedges and saplings that passed for countryside in the borough. Even in the shroud of night, all three figures cast distinctive silhouettes: one tall and skinny, one small and round, while the huge outline of the third was crowned by a magnificent stovepipe hat.

Arthur paused from rubbing boot polish into his face to give Carnegie a peevish look. "Couldn't you at least leave the hat in the carriage?"

"Someone might steal it! Anyway, where I go, the hat goes."

The reporter sighed, and put the boot polish back into a shapeless bag hanging from his shoulder. "We might as well make a start. The moon's behind some fairly thick cloud cover, which should help us."

Carnegie looked at Arthur with interest. "Since when have you been an expert on burglary?"

He shrugged. "I'm a reporter. Sometimes you've got to go that extra bit further to get a scoop."

"What, into people's bedrooms?"

"I have in the past. After all, it was how I solved the mystery of the kidnapped Wilberforce twins. What's so funny?"

Jonathan was unsuccessfully trying to stifle a laugh. "I'm sorry, Arthur. It's just that . . . well, you don't exactly look like your average burglar."

The reporter glared at him. "I was breaking into mansions on Savage Row while you were still soiling diapers. You just worry about yourself." He consulted Marianne's note again. "Now, if the bounty hunter's right, de Quincy's house should back onto these woods here. Follow me, and try to watch where you're putting your feet."

Arthur moved into the woodland with surprising stealth, while Carnegie padded silently along behind him. In contrast, Jonathan had to concentrate on each footstep, trying to avoid treading on the brittle twigs and crackling leaves. Around him, tendrils of mist drifted dolefully around slender tree trunks. Removed from the factories and chimney stacks that dominated the center of Darkside, the air in the woods was cleaner and crisper than Jonathan was used to. His breath made frosty patterns in the air.

He was beginning to lose track of the time they had spent tiptoeing through the woods when suddenly Carnegie placed a warning hand on his arm. Through the darkness, Jonathan could discern a high stone wall looming up in front of them. The woodland had been cleared from around it, preventing anyone from gaining easy access via the trees. If the edifice was not imposing enough, sharpened spikes had been placed on top of the wall.

Carnegie shook his head. "De Quincy *really* doesn't want any visitors."

Arthur reached into his bag and pulled out a length of rope, attached to a small grappling hook. "I imagine the wall's the least of our problems," he said.

Paying out a length of rope for himself, he swung the grappling hook around in a couple of practice arcs before casting it up and over the wall. With a cold, clinking sound, the grapple caught on one of the spikes and stuck in place. Carnegie nodded with approval.

"Nice shot. You're wasted on journalism."

Arthur spat on both hands, took a firm grasp of the rope, and began to climb. Jonathan looked on, open-mouthed. He would never have thought it possible, but somehow the reporter was able to haul his bulky frame up the wall. Arthur's arms had to be remarkably strong. Jonathan was reminded what a dangerous life he led, and how many assassination attempts he had survived. At times it was easy to underestimate the reporter, but beneath the rolls of flesh lay a will of iron.

At the top of the wall, Arthur maneuvered himself into a perched position between two of the spikes. He checked that the coast was clear before nodding to Carnegie, who pulled himself up with ease. Jonathan took a deep breath, and began his ascent. He had never been the most adept at gym in school, and the mist had made the rope slippery. One step at a time, however, his feet sought out footholds in the wall, and he found himself making slow but steady progress up it. Eventually the spikes hovered into view, and a strong arm was lifting him into a sitting position.

"Not bad for a first time," said Carnegie.

Jonathan nodded, too out of breath to reply. Beside him, Arthur was peering out over the grounds like the lookout on a pirate ship. Jonathan followed his gaze.

"What on earth is that?" he breathed.

Before them loomed a circular domed structure in the middle of a vast expanse of gravel. Forbidding metal walls rose high up into the air. A dead shell of a building, it was lined with rows and rows of blank windows, many with smashed panes. No lights were visible anywhere.

"Of course!" Arthur replied. "The Panopticon!"

"Pan-what?"

"Panopticon. It's a kind of prison. It was built by the authorities before Darkside was cut off from the rest of London. They thought it might help cut the crime rate, but it didn't work."

"Why not?"

Arthur gave him a sideways look. "Darksiders aren't huge fans of prisons. There were so many people on the outside trying to help the prisoners escape that the place fell under siege. The wardens ran away when Darkside was founded, and it's been out of use ever since. To be honest, I'd forgotten it existed."

Jonathan examined the foreboding structure again. "And Marianne thinks de Quincy *lives* here?"

The reporter shrugged. "It's not exactly homey, but you can bet it's secure. Shall we go and investigate?"

Out of the corner of his eye, Jonathan noticed something moving. "Hang on a minute. What's that there?"

He pointed at two shapes bounding across the grounds in their direction.

"Oh. Dogs," said Arthur. "I don't like dogs."

To Jonathan's mind, the word *dogs* didn't really do justice to the beasts galloping toward them. They were nearly the size of small ponies, and their movements rippled with a muscular ferocity. With every bark they displayed slavering jaws bursting with teeth. On reaching the section of the wall the three intruders were balancing upon, the hounds began pawing at it, their claws ripping chunks out of the brickwork. Jonathan drew back in horror. One slip now, and he would be torn to shreds.

Without a word, Carnegie dropped down from the wall, one hand clamping his hat down onto his head, and his overcoat flapping like bat wings in the breeze around him. As the wereman landed, the beasts made to lunge at him, only to pause in bewilderment. They stopped barking and pawing. One sniffed him gingerly, and then nuzzled his leg with its head.

Carnegie looked up at his companions, smiling. "Come on. It's all right. They're crossbreeds — half wolf. They won't hurt you while I'm here."

Arthur lowered the rope down the other side of the wall and climbed down to the ground. After a dubious pause, so did Jonathan. The hounds eyed them both with interest, but no malice. Carnegie stroked the dog on his left-hand side.

"See? They're fine."

At that moment the moon was unveiled from behind the clouds. The grounds of the Panopticon were bathed with a pale light, which picked out a silhouette moving along the skyline.

"What on Darkside . . . ?" muttered Carnegie.

A figure was swinging arm over arm across a rope that stretched between the perimeter wall and the Panopticon. Despite the fact that one false move would send him hurtling to his death, he moved through the air with the graceful ease of a ballerina.

"It's that guy from the Cain Club!" Jonathan exclaimed.

"Impressive," Carnegie said grudgingly. "In a showy sort of way."

"But if he's the murderer, we've got to get inside right now! Come on!"

Jonathan set off like a greyhound toward the building, his feet biting into the gravel. Focused on the Panopticon, he dimly registered the presence of Carnegie and the hounds hurtling along near him, and heard Arthur wheezing painfully at the rear. The gravel seemed to go on endlessly, and Jonathan ran till his lungs burned and his legs ached. Above his head, the intruder swung almost lazily along the rope, narrowing the gap to the dome of the prison with every stretch.

Suddenly Jonathan was under the cold shadow of the Panopticon. Up close, the prison was even more forbidding. Constructed on a foundation of desperation and madness, it had none of the dreadful elegance of other buildings in Darkside. In years gone by, the pockmarked walls had repelled outsiders as mercilessly as they had trapped the screams of its inmates. Now they stood impassively silent. The front entrance was a thick metal door, whose primary function was to deny entry rather than allow it.

Jonathan shook his head and turned to see Carnegie and the hounds jogging up to him.

"This place is a fortress. Can we go through one of the windows?" he asked.

The wereman shook his head. "They're cells. You'd just end up behind bars. We'll have to go through the front door."

Carnegie sized up the metal entrance and made as if to shoulder-charge it, when a ragged shout behind him pulled him up short.

"Wait!"

Arthur staggered up to them, exhausted. "You'll never get in that way. Let me try."

Dipping back inside his bag, the reporter pulled out a leather pouch containing a set of long, thin pieces of metal. He got down onto his knees and began inserting different combinations into the lock. Looking upward, Jonathan saw the intruder reach the end of the rope and haul himself onto the side of the dome.

"Hurry, Arthur!"

The reporter grimaced. "This isn't any ordinary lock. It's going to take a bit of time."

Sweat was running down Arthur's face like a waterfall. He paused to mop his forehead with a handkerchief, and then attacked the lock with renewed vigor. Slipping one wire into the top of the lock, he jiggled a second around in the bottom, hoping to catch the mechanism.

Carnegie growled with frustration. "We haven't got all night."

"Well, if you just let me concentrate I might be able to . . ."

There was a loud click.

"Gotcha!" Arthur cried.

The door swung open to reveal a dark corridor leading deeper into the heart of the Panopticon. The hounds sniffed the dank air cautiously, and then took several paces backward. Jonathan glanced nervously at Arthur.

"That's not a good sign."

From inside the building there was a prolonged bloodcurdling scream, and the definitive report of a pistol.

17

They made their way slowly and carefully along the corridor. For all their previous haste, no one seemed inclined to run now. Carnegie led the way through the dark, quietly sharpening his claws on the sides of the passage. Jonathan shivered and drew his jacket more tightly around him. The corridor was icily cold, and the freezing air assailed the softest and most exposed parts of his skin: his cheeks, his earlobes, the tips of his fingers.

There had been no more screams or gunshots. Jonathan's footsteps echoed guiltily on the flagstones. He wondered what the mysterious intruder's intentions were, and whether de Quincy was now just a lifeless corpse somewhere inside the Panopticon. Bodies seemed to be piling up at every turn. The link between the Ripper James's death and his mom's disappearance at times seemed such a fragile one that Jonathan feared that at any moment they would hit a dead end in their investigation. Was this the closest he was going to get to uncovering the truth?

A light was flickering up ahead, and he could see that the corridor led out into a large room. Carnegie flattened himself against the side of the wall and shuffled forward, gesturing at his companions to follow his example. Jonathan edged forward toward the light, pressing his skin to the freezing stonework. Alongside him, Arthur tried to flatten his bulky frame against the wall. At the end of the corridor, the wereman peered around the corner for a few seconds, and then stalked out of the shadows. Jonathan gave Arthur a worried look, but the journalist merely shrugged in reply. There wasn't any option: The two followed Carnegie into the open.

Jonathan's first impression was one of a vast space. He was standing at the edge of a dome formed by an enormous honeycomb of cells and gangways that ran around the walls of the building. There must have been hundreds of cells arranged in neat rows one on top of the other, each one caged off behind a latticework of iron bars. Jonathan strained to see if there was anyone still trapped in the cells, but they all appeared to be empty. On the ground floor, flaming torches writhed in the arctic drafts, only able to cast their illumination up a handful of levels. Somewhere near the roof, the occasional chirp and sound of fluttering hinted at the presence of bats nestling in the eaves.

In the center of the space there was a tall column that stretched up nearly all the way to the ceiling of the dome, topped off with an observation room dominated by large, shuttered windows. The room must have been where the guards had worked when the Panopticon had still been packed with prisoners. From that lofty vantage point, Jonathan thought he could have seen into any of the cells. The brooding structure only served to heighten the air of desolation within the building.

It was at that moment, looking up, that Jonathan saw a figure falling from the top of the watchtower.

Nicholas nearly hadn't noticed the intruder at all. He had been busy in the watchtower, composing an elegant blackmail letter to a rich Darkside lady who had been cheating on her husband. Over the years Nicholas had discovered that he could run the family business just as easily from the confines of the Panopticon as from the center of the borough. The observation room had been converted into a plush study, where the shelves were packed with old correspondences, letters containing angry threats and strenuous denials, letters pleading penury, letters begging for silence. Nicholas's study was an epicenter of evil that sent waves of fear and guilt rolling out over Darkside.

He was signing off with a flourish when he heard a small metallic noise on the roof above him. Nicholas put down his quill and headed over to the window, where he peered through the shutters. The Panopticon was as still and dismal as ever. He was about to return to his desk when a movement up in the eaves caught his eye. Straining his eyes, Nicholas was shocked to make out a figure clambering down a wire toward the observation room. The noise must have been the sound of some sort of grapple attaching itself to the watchtower. Whoever this brash intruder was, they clearly meant business.

Nicholas moved back from the window and reached into the drawer of his writing desk, pulling out a pistol. As always, it was cleaned and ready to fire. Crucially, the intruder had lost the element of surprise. Breaking into the Panopticon was one thing; hunting down Nicholas de Quincy was another. Years ago he had taken the precaution of building a secret passageway in the floor of the watchtower that ran half a mile underground to nearby stables, where a carriage and team of fast horses was on permanent standby. Nicholas would be back on the Grand before the intruder had managed to break into his study. In the meantime, a group of thugs would be heading in the opposite direction to deal with the rude interruption.

Nicholas gave a thin smile of triumph as he gathered up a sheaf of his most lucrative correspondences and headed for the door. Daydreaming of the intruder's violent demise, it was a complete surprise when a winged beast came crashing through the windows directly *behind* him. De Quincy spun around, only to see the creature land easily on the floor, an infernal combination of razor-sharp teeth and talons. The lights in the study went out. He screamed, and fired a shot.

Jonathan couldn't move, couldn't breathe, couldn't tear his eyes away. The figure falling from the watchtower was the man they had seen swinging through the air toward the Panopticon, now a jumble of arms and legs and torn black clothing hurtling toward a bone-shattering impact on the flagstones. As Jonathan gazed on in horror, the man dragged something from his pocket and hurled it at the watchtower. The device bit into the brickwork, and in the blink of an eye his free fall was brought to a jarring halt and he was swinging in a wide arc from a wire.

Carnegie let out a low whistle.

"Lucky devil."

A loud, inhuman screech rang out from the observation room.

"What on Darkside was that?" gasped Arthur.

"Whatever it was, it wasn't Nicholas de Quincy," replied Jonathan. "Carnegie?"

The wereman was gazing up at the watchtower, an apprehensive look on his face. Then he said, in a quiet voice: "Split up. I'll try to draw it out of here."

"Draw what?"

There was another screech from the observation room, and a bank of black cloud came billowing out of a broken window.

"MOVE!" bellowed Carnegie, shoving Jonathan in the shoulder.

Jonathan stayed where he was, transfixed by the approaching dark cloud. It was a shadow that cradled a horrible threat, the kind of darkness that had lain underneath Jonathan's bed and in the cracks between wardrobe doors when he was a child. As the cloud neared, he heard the sound of beating wings from within it, and suddenly the torches around them spluttered and winked out, submerging the Panopticon in night.

From somewhere in the darkness, Carnegie bellowed a primeval challenge, which was answered by another piercing shriek. Then there was the sound of a brutal collision, and the wereman howled in pain. Jonathan was desperate to run, but his legs had turned to jelly. Then he realized that the sounds of fighting had broken off.

"Down, boy!" Carnegie shouted. "It's coming for you!"

Instinctively, Jonathan hurled himself to the ground, and there was a *whoosh* as something sliced through the air where he had been standing. He hadn't even heard the creature flying toward him.

Spread-eagled on his stomach, Jonathan crawled over the flagstones toward the nearest wall. He couldn't see or hear anything. There was another *whoosh*, and he felt a gust on his face as the thing flew low over the ground past him. Scrabbling blindly for some sort of weapon, Jonathan felt his fingers close in on the cold steel of a cell door. One of the bars had been dislodged, giving him just enough room to slip through. There was another screech, this time impossibly close. Jonathan didn't hesitate, wriggling through the gap and throwing himself to the back of the cell.

A second later the bars rang out as the creature battered itself against them. An overpowering smell of rotting meat flooded into the cell. Even so close, Jonathan couldn't see the creature through the darkness, but he could hear the high-pitched ringing of its talons against iron, and the brutal war cries it made as it fought to break through. The walls of the cell seemed to shudder beneath the force of the assault.

Jonathan pressed himself against the back wall of the cell and began tugging at the bars that ran across the window. The rattling and shrieking behind him got louder and louder, until he thought either his eardrums would burst or he would go crazy. Then, as quickly as it had appeared, the smell of sour flesh vanished, and the sound died away. Jonathan could hear the beating of leathery wings as they rose toward the higher levels of the Panopticon.

Jonathan slumped down into a heap. He wanted to cry, but he just felt empty. He put his head in his hands, and didn't lift it again until a voice said:

"There you are."

Carnegie was standing by the cage door, a lit torch in his hand. His face was scratched and bleeding, but apart from that he appeared unharmed. "It's all right, boy. It's gone."

Jonathan looked up at the wereman. "That was unbelievable," he said, in a daze. "I was so *scared*."

"I think we all were." Arthur popped up from behind Carnegie's shoulder. "It's safe now, though."

Jonathan eased himself through the bars and back out into the Panopticon. Carnegie walked over to the watchtower and held up his torch, exposing the wire hanging lifelessly down from the side of the structure. The intruder was nowhere to be seen.

"It seems our mysterious friend has made another escape."

"I wouldn't quite say that," Arthur replied thoughtfully. "Before that creature appeared, I caught a glimpse of his face."

"Did you recognize him?"

"You could say so. After all, I do work with him. It was Harry Pierce."

18

Raquella was asleep in her quarters when he came for her. Her dreams were restless visions, and when the door creaked open she was immediately awake. She sat up quickly, drawing the covers around her. Against the backdrop of the lit corridor was the silhouette of Vendetta, leaning heavily on a cane for support. Though she was unsettled by this unprecedented visit, she adopted an assertive, almost resentful tone.

"It is late, sir. What can I do for you?"

Vendetta wheezed softly.

"I am walking again," he announced thickly. "For the first time in weeks, I can use my legs. I thought you might want to know."

"Naturally, I am delighted, sir. Forgive me, but it is late and I was sleeping. Perhaps in the morning I would be more responsive."

A hint of a smile appeared on Vendetta's face. "Are you developing subtlety, Raquella?"

It was the first time he had used her name in a long while. She didn't like the way it sounded in his mouth.

"I suppose it should be encouraged . . . up to a point. I haven't woken you merely to display my improvement, though that should be reason enough. No, there's a secret I want to share with you. I don't know how you're going to react, but I thought it would be rather fun to find out."

Raquella's fingers tightened around the covers. Vendetta's moods were becoming increasingly erratic. She wondered if the poison had spread to his brain, and driven him slightly mad. Or had he always been this way, and she had been too cowed to notice?

"I would be honored to learn this secret, sir, but could it not wait until morning?"

The vampire lifted up his cane and swept it across Raquella's dressing table, sending hairpins, family photographs, and toiletries crashing onto the wooden floorboards. The maid winced at the sound of breaking glass.

"You'll get up now or I'll beat you where you lie," spat Vendetta. Then he paused, and a softer mood seemed to wash over him. "I'll wait outside while you dress. Do not take long."

And with that, he shut the bedroom door.

Shivering, Raquella pulled on some clothes and joined her master outside her room. It was half past four in the morning, and the drafty corridors of Vendetta Heights were still and cold. Outside, she could hear the wind angrily buffeting the side of the house. The only other sound was the tapping of Vendetta's cane on the floor. His ancestors glared down from their portraits on the walls. Raquella could almost hear them thinking: *What is he doing, spending time with a mere servant girl? She's not fit to clean his silverware.* But then, Raquella was well aware that Vendetta played by his own rules, not anyone else's.

They walked on toward the west wing of Vendetta Heights. It was the part of the building reserved for guests, and had lain empty ever since Raquella had started work. To her surprise, she noted that someone had lit the gas lamps in the corridor. Vendetta ignored the entrance to the main hall that dominated the wing and moved on to an unassuming door farther down the corridor. Expertly selecting the right key from a huge bunch in his pocket, he slipped inside and beckoned for her to follow.

Beyond the door was a cubbyhole rather than a room, with barely enough space for two people to stand. The air was filled with the sound of Vendetta's ragged breaths and the rustling of Raquella's clothing. She was suddenly uncomfortably aware of the vampire's proximity, his breath as cold as a tombstone on her neck. Two eyeholes had been cut into the wall, which, the maid realized, looked out onto the main hall.

"My ancestors were a suspicious lot," said Vendetta quietly. "I don't think there's a room in the building you can't spy on in one fashion or another. Not that I usually bother with such nonsense, but, as you'll see, tonight things are rather different."

Raquella realized that he was waiting for her to look through the eyeholes. Her heart racing, she pressed her face to the wall. The lights beyond were dimmed, shrouding the depths of the room in secrecy. The only illumination came from the great fire, which raged away against the darkness. Standing in front of the hearth, hands clasped behind his back as he stared dolefully into the flames, was William Joubert.

Raquella gasped.

"Father? But how?"

"William came to me last night, saying he was in trouble and in need of shelter. I chose to open my door to him."

"He came *here* for help?"

"William and I share a certain . . . history. He was supposed to work for me many years ago, until circumstances intervened. Did it never occur to you that we might know each other? Of all the girls in Darkside, why do you think I hired you? Why do you think you are still alive?"

Raquella's head spun. Her meek and gentle father and her vicious master knew each other? What set of circumstances could ever have brought them together? In one sense, it was irrelevant. William was safe and hidden away in the last place in Darkside that anyone would ever think to look for him. Maybe there was a way her family could stay together, after all.

"You have no idea what this will mean to my mother. Sir, this is an act of great kindness."

Vendetta smiled cruelly. "Well, not *quite*," he said. "You

see, whoever is hunting your father will be watching your mother like a hawk. If she began making regular trips up to the Heights, it wouldn't take them long to put two and two together. I can't allow that. My hospitality stretches only so far."

"Are you saying I can't tell mother that father is here?"

"Oh, you can tell her. But I'll never let her in the house, and if she even tries to gain entry, things will rapidly turn ugly."

Raquella looked at her father, torn. "Why?" she said bitterly.

Vendetta took hold of her chin and turned it firmly upward until her face met his. She felt herself chill under the icy gaze of his blue eyes.

"Understand this. I could have let your father stay out in the cold until he was hunted down like a dog and murdered. The only reason he is alive is because I let him in, and such a deed does not come without its risks to myself. And given my current condition . . ." He looked away. "I am what I am, Raquella. This is as close to thanks as you will ever get."

It was such a struggle to take it all in. Raquella didn't know whether to feel happy or sad, grateful or angry.

Which, she guessed, was what Vendetta had intended all along. Again, she reached inside herself and found the calm assurance that had kept her alive through years of dangerous service.

"May I speak to him?" she asked briskly.

"Be my guest," Vendetta replied. "Your father is."

19

"OK, boy, you can come in now."

Jonathan turned the door handle and entered the observation room. He found himself in a study that had recently witnessed a violent struggle. Furniture had been upturned, and one of the bookshelves had been toppled onto the floor. Icy winds swooped in through smashed windows. Worse, Jonathan couldn't help noticing several long streaks of blood running across the floor.

Amid the disorder, Arthur Blake was sitting down behind a desk, a gray expression on his face. Carnegie stood with his back to the room and his hands folded behind his back, staring out of one of the windows. Near the door, a long cloak had been placed over a shapeless mass. Jonathan nodded at the mound.

"De Quincy?"

"Let's just say he won't be writing any more nasty letters," replied Arthur humorlessly.

"Was it . . . I mean, did it look the same as the others?"

The reporter nodded.

"Well, it can't have been Harry. I don't know what he was up to, but he couldn't rip a man apart. What *was* that thing, Carnegie?" Jonathan asked.

The wereman didn't bother to turn around. "Doesn't matter what it was," he replied curtly. "It was very big, very fast, and very dangerous. What else do you need to know?"

"But what about the black cloud?"

"Enough, boy!" Carnegie yelled. "Can't you leave it alone?"

Jonathan bit back a sharp reply. Ever since the three of them had regrouped, Carnegie had been withdrawn and sullen. There was a look in his eyes that Jonathan had never seen before. If he didn't know better, he would have called it fear.

"We're too late, then," he said glumly.

"Not necessarily," Arthur replied, rising briskly. "De

Quincy may be gone, but we're in his private study. Let's see if we can find anything useful."

The portly reporter began searching the wrecked room, pulling files down from the shelves and rummaging through drawers. Eager to take his mind off the nearby corpse, Jonathan lent a hand, leaving Carnegie to stand where he was.

After ten minutes of leafing through de Quincy's correspondences, Jonathan groaned with frustration.

"Have you seen how many of these things he's written? Was there anyone he wasn't blackmailing?"

Arthur gave him a grim look. "This is Darkside, Jonathan. Everyone's got a secret."

"Yeah, but this is going to take forever."

He felt a tap on his shoulder, and looked around to see Carnegie brandishing a neat black folder. There was a bloodstain on the top-left corner.

"Whatever you're looking for will probably be in here. He was carrying it when he was killed."

"Oh. Er, thanks," Jonathan replied, gingerly taking the folder at arm's length.

He quickly carried it over to the desk and emptied its contents out over the surface. Then he and Arthur began shuffling through the papers. Jonathan was reading a lengthy threat to a Darkside businessman who was secretly double-crossing his partner when the reporter let out a low whistle.

"Bingo. See the date on this? That was last week. And see who it's addressed to."

Jonathan took the paper and began to read.

MY DEAREST BROTHER FLEET,

IT HAS BEEN MANY YEARS SINCE WE LAST SPOKE. WHILE YOU HAVE NO DOUBT GRIEVED FOR THE PLEASURE OF MY COMPANY, GIVEN OUR RATHER FRAUGHT EXPERIENCES ALL THOSE YEARS BEFORE, A PARTING OF THE WAYS SEEMED VERY NECESSARY. I TRUST YOU HAVE FULLY RECOVERED YOUR WITS FOLLOWING THE UNPLEASANTNESS REGARDING YOUR LATE, LAMENTED BROTHER JAMES.

SO WHY, I HEAR YOU THINKING, HAS MY OLD BROTHER SEEN FIT TO CONTACT ME AGAIN NOW? THE TRUTH IS, THERE HAS BEEN A REUNION OF SORTS AMONG THE GENTLEMEN. BROTHERS SPINE AND RAKE HAVE JOINED ME IN A NEW BUSINESS

VENTURE THAT WE THOUGHT YOU SHOULD HEAR ABOUT. WE HAVE COME INTO THE POSSESSION OF SOME FASCINATING INFORMATION REGARDING THE REAL IDENTITY OF YOUR SOLE SURVIVING SIBLING. THIS MEANS THAT WE ARE THE ONLY PEOPLE IN DARKSIDE — BARRING THOMAS RIPPER HIMSELF "MAY HIS HEALTH NEVER FAIL HIM" — WHO KNOW BOTH THE RIPPER HEIRS. PLAYING STRAIGHT AS EVER, I HAVE WRITTEN TO BOTH OF YOU WITH THIS OFFER: WHICHEVER ONE OF YOU PAYS US THE MOST MONEY SHALL BE GRANTED THE IDENTITY OF THE OTHER. THIS WOULD ALLOW YOU TO DISPATCH YOUR SIBLING NOW, THEREBY AVOIDING ANY POTENTIAL MESSINESS WITH A BLOOD SUCCESSION — AN ADVANTAGE I'M SURE YOU WERE AWARE OF WHEN YOU BUMPED OLD JAMES OFF. AREN'T YOU GLAD NOW YOU ASKED US TO HELP YOU?

YOU HAVE SEVEN DAYS TO MAKE US AN OFFER.

YOURS FRATERNALLY,

BROTHER HEART

"It's a copy," said Arthur, reading over his shoulder. "Our friend Nicholas was nothing if not meticulous."

"He was blackmailing Brother Fleet?"

"It's bigger than that," the reporter replied excitedly. "According to this letter, Brother Fleet wasn't just any old Gentleman. He was a Ripper, too! Of course! It's all starting to make sense now."

"OK," Jonathan said slowly. "So Nicholas managed to get the rest of the Gentlemen to gang up on Brother Fleet. But how did he think he was going to get away with blackmailing one Ripper, let alone two?"

"Maybe he thought he was safe here," Carnegie growled softly from the window. "Maybe he just didn't care anymore. Look around you, boy. Can you imagine staring out of this window every day? What do you think that does to a man?"

Jonathan looked out over the Panopticon. In every direction there was the dark grotto of a cell, a hundred tiny prisons of human misery. He shivered, but not from the cold this time.

"Let's get out of here," he muttered. "Where do we go now?"

"Back to the newspaper," replied Arthur. "We've got some news for our esteemed editor."

The angry cry echoed around the dusty main office of *The Informer*. Even down in the basement, where the printers were half-deafened by the ceaseless clatter of the presses, they looked up from their machines and wondered which prominent citizen had threatened to kill them all this time, or how large an expense claim a reporter had just handed in. For the thousandth time, they questioned what they were doing working in such a dangerous trade. Petty theft or embezzlement would be a cinch compared to this.

"Harry?" shrieked Lucien. "Are you sure?"

His indignant shouts were overtaken by a hacking cough that made him double over as if he had been shot in the belly. Perched precariously on the edge of Arthur's cluttered desk, the sickly editor looked paler and more tired than ever. At that moment, he seemed to be surviving on anger alone.

Jonathan nodded.

"That little wretch!" Lucien coughed. "I'll throttle him!"

"Ahem . . ." interjected Arthur. "There's probably a couple of questions we could ask him *before* you kill him . . ."

"I don't care! He tried to bash my brains in at the Cain Club! And after all I've done for him!"

"Rant and rave on your own time," Carnegie growled. "I haven't slept for a while, and I'm feeling tetchy. When are you expecting the boy in?"

Jonathan was rather relieved to hear the wereman reverting to his usual bullish demeanor. The strange mood that had taken over him in the Panopticon had receded, though he was still quieter than usual.

"Actually, I haven't seen him for a couple of days," Lucien admitted, dabbing at his mouth with a handkerchief. "Apparently he's been too busy impersonating a master thief to show up at the office. I almost hope for his sake he doesn't come back."

"Where does he live?"

"Haven't the faintest idea. He was cheap, and — till recently — he came to work on time. That was all I cared about." He rubbed his face with his hand. "OK, so where are we now?"

Arthur methodically ticked off his fingers. "One: James Arkel was murdered by his brother. Two: His sibling was known as Brother Fleet, and was a member of a group known as the Gentlemen. Three: Some of the Gentlemen had discovered the identity of Fleet's other sibling, and were playing them off against one another. Four: They're now all dead."

"Not exactly surprising," Lucien murmured.

"Indeed. Five: The only other surviving member of the Gentlemen is William Joubert — Brother Steel, by my logic — who's gone into hiding."

"He's the key," said Carnegie slowly. "If he's still alive, we have to find him before Brother Fleet does."

"Easier said than done. If Raquella has no idea where her father's gone, how are we supposed to know?"

As the conversation drifted on, Jonathan retreated into himself. His muscles were aching, and he was still recovering from the horror inspired by the creature in the Panopticon. All he wanted to do was to go back to Lightside, crawl into bed, and sleep for a week, leaving blackmail and brutal murders far behind him. At that moment in time, even school seemed preferable to this.

The old Lightside newspaper from his mom's drawer was sitting on Arthur's desk. Jonathan idly picked it up and began flicking it through it, taking a peculiar comfort from old news stories, problem pages, and soccer scores. On the other side of the room Carnegie and Arthur were having a heated argument about what to do next. He wasn't sure why they bothered. They had hit another brick wall, William was in all likelihood already dead, and that was that.

As he dragged his eyes wearily over the classifieds he saw that one of the advertisements had been circled in red pen. Jonathan's blood froze, and he sat bolt upright in his chair. Right there in front of him, tastefully framed in a black box, was the following:

The Prometheus Gallery is proud to unveil a new col-lection of works by artists Cal Rufus, Lorna Klein, and Edwin Spine. Open six days a week, from 9:30 A.M. to 4:30 P.M.

He glanced at the date of the Lightside newspaper. It was dated two months after James's death. Maybe they hadn't hit a dead end after all.

Carnegie broke off from haranguing Arthur and gave him a shrewd look. "Seen something exciting there, boy?"

Jonathan stared numbly at the page in front of him. "Reading the papers . . . My dad said they were having a coffee and reading the papers, and then Mom went really quiet. I think this was the paper she was reading."

The wereman came over and cast an eye over the front page. "Well, the date fits."

"And look here." Jonathan spread the newspaper out on the desk. "She circled this ad. Any of those names look familiar to you?"

Suddenly Arthur was on his shoulder. "I'm guessing Edwin Spine is our old friend Mr. Rafferty."

"He was displaying his paintings. But not in Darkside, in Lightside! And my mom found out. Don't you see? She went to the exhibition and saw something that sent her racing back to Darkside." Jonathan turned to Carnegie, his eyes shining. "And I'll bet you all the money in the world it had to do with James Arkel."

20

Crossing was easier now. His body still trembled when he passed that invisible boundary, his heartbeat still fluttered like the wings of a hummingbird, but his mind was calmer, more certain. He was becoming more comfortable with the waxing and waning of the two worlds he inhabited. Jonathan may not have been truly from either Darkside or Lightside, but he could survive in both places. As he came out blinking into the crispness of a London winter morning, he felt a sense of freedom blossoming within him.

Unable to face the long journey to Lone Square, Jonathan had badgered Carnegie into showing him a different route back to Lightside. Reluctantly, the wereman had agreed. He led Jonathan north of the Grand and up the crest of a steep hill that broke out into a scrubby patch of parkland. It was a dismal sight, devoid of life and color. Instead, the wind sliced through brown, overgrown grasses and weeds. A dank pond sat sullenly over to Jonathan's left. There was no one around.

Carnegie stomped through the grass, heading toward a tangled thicket beyond the pond.

"I've used this crossing point a couple of times. It comes out on Hampstead Heath in your London."

"Good. That's near the gallery." Jonathan stopped. "It's not that far from my house either. Why didn't we go this way last time?"

The wereman stopped and looked at him sharply, wiping his nose on his sleeve. "Oh, I'm sorry, boy. Have I been slowing you down?" he said acidly.

"I didn't mean it like that," Jonathan protested. "It just seems funny that you're showing me this one now, that's all."

"You cross when and where I tell you, boy. This place is only safe now because the gang of cutthroats who usually ply their trade here have holed themselves up in the Silver Cage. I know that because I saw them go in there earlier today, and when those boys start drinking, they don't stop for a couple of days. Everything I do, I do for a reason. Understand?"

Jonathan nodded.

"Good. Go in a straight line through that thicket there. The park should still be clear when you return, but don't dawdle."

And with that, Carnegie turned on his heel and thrashed his way back through the undergrowth. Jonathan took a few tentative steps into the thicket, muttering to himself about the wereman's temper. Dried twigs and leaves crunched beneath his feet. Brambles tore at his clothing and his skin, tough and sharp as barbed wire. But then, with surprising suddenness, it came to an end, and Jonathan was extricating himself from the other side of the thicket, passing Londoners out running or walking their dogs.

Hampstead Heath had been one of his favorite haunts when he was younger, and he knew the rolling pathways like the back of his hand. On a couple of occasions, his father had brought him up here for long, rambling walks. Those had been some of the few times they had spent any time together, though they walked in silence on Alain's insistence. That seemed a long time ago, now. Everything had changed.

Now he was back on Lightside, it was tempting to head east and visit home again. But Jonathan knew that he would have to go over what he had discovered, and Alain would have so many questions, and Mrs. Elwood so many objections, that there just wasn't enough time. Also, Alain would have insisted that he come along to the gallery, and he wasn't well enough yet. Dimly, Jonathan realized that his mom had made the same choice all those years ago, and had vanished with only an answering machine message left behind. Would he, too, now vanish into thin air?

So instead, Jonathan slipped off the Heath at the south side, jogging down Parliament Hill and down into the genteel center of Hampstead, where cafés and shops sat placidly in the sunshine. He was relieved to see the Prometheus Art Gallery was still at the same address. The name was painted in gold lettering over a black storefront. Watercolors of stormy seascapes rested on easels in the window.

Jonathan went through the front door, and into a low-ceilinged room with wooden floorboards. A handful of paintings were hanging from the long, whitewashed walls. An elderly man was standing behind the counter flicking through a catalog, a pair of half-moon glasses perched on his nose. He looked up as Jonathan entered, and gave him an appraising look.

"May I help you?" he asked, in the tone that adults in shops often used when they addressed Jonathan: part patronizing, part bored, and just a few seconds away from phoning the police.

"Hi," Jonathan replied awkwardly. "I wanted to ask you about an exhibition you had here. Er . . . twelve years ago."

"Good grief!" The art dealer took off his glasses. "It's unlikely that I'll be able to remember that far back, young man, but I'll try my best. What was the name of the exhibition?"

"There were three painters: Cal Rufus, Lorna Klein, and . . . Edwin Spine."

If Jonathan had been hoping for a reaction, he certainly got one. At the mention of Edwin's name, the old man jumped as if he had been scalded. He tapped his fingers on the counter, pretending to think, and trying to regain his composure.

"Now, let me see," he said, pressing his fingers to his lips. "Yes, that does ring some faint bells . . ."

"It's Edwin Spine I'm interested in," Jonathan pressed. "Have you still got any of his paintings?"

The art dealer leaned over the counter. "And why would you be interested in that *particular* artist?"

Jonathan stared back at him, unflinching. "My mom's a fan," he said. "Have you got any or not?"

The old man *ummed* and *ahhed* before seeming to arrive at a decision. He folded his glasses away in a case and led Jonathan deeper into the gallery, continuing to talk in an accent that tinkled like crystal.

"As luck would have it, our collection of Spines does still reside here. I have to say, it's very unusual to be asked about him. Your mother must be a lady with very refined taste. . . ."

Beyond the watercolors was a room filled with sculptures. Jonathan realized that the gallery was deceptively large. A grotesque marble statue of a gargoyle caught his eye as they passed toward a door in the far wall. The dealer unlocked it, and let Jonathan inside a storeroom jammed with packing crates. The sparse illumination emitting from a lone bulb was in sharp contrast to the soft mood lighting in the rest of the gallery. The dealer threaded his way to the back of the room, and stopped at a dusty, warped crate.

"If memory serves me correctly, the Spines should be in this case here."

He was prizing off the lid when suddenly the door banged open, and the large figure of Correlli barged into the storeroom. Dressed in his habitual open waistcoat, there was a grim look in the showman's eyes that Jonathan had never seen before. The dealer gave him a peevish look.

"Excuse me, sir, but this room is private. I must ask you to leave."

By way of reply, the fire-eater kicked the door shut behind him, stalked over to the old man, and gave him a resounding backhand slap across the face. The dealer crumpled to the floor. Jonathan made to run but Correlli pulled out a small, silver pistol and pointed it at him.

"You so much as twitch and I'll put a bullet in you. It's been a long journey over here and I've had to hurry. I'm not going to let you slink off now."

Jonathan gasped. "But . . . how did you know?"

"My employer had a little word in my ear. There's not much that gets past him. You know how to make some powerful enemies, Jonathan."

There was a whimper from the floor.

"Please, whoever you are," said the dealer. "Don't hurt me!"

Correlli made as if to slap him again, and then stopped short. He peered closely at the old man's face.

"Where have I seen you before?" the fire-eater murmured. "There's something very familiar about you."

"I don't know what you're talking about. Please let me go!"

"Sol something . . . Sol Byrne, isn't it? You used to work with Lorcan Bracket years back. I never forget a face, Sol. You're a long way from Darkside."

When the old man answered, it was no longer in the posh, rich tones of before, but the nasal gutterspeak that Jonathan heard every day on the Grand.

"'Aven't used that name in a long time, and I 'aven't been back in Darkside for years. I'm different now. I'm straight, respectable."

Correlli broke out into a mocking laugh.

"'Respectable'? Hardly. No matter how fancy your surroundings, you're still a common crook, Sol. You reek of grubby little thefts. Now, what are you doing here?"

"Please . . . Mr. Rafferty, sir, Edwin. He hired me to keep this shop open, to sell his paintings. The boy here was asking about 'em."

"Is that so?" As the fire-eater glanced around the room, Jonathan half thought about making a break for the door, but it was useless. It was twenty feet away, and Correlli's pistol was still trained on him. He wouldn't make it out alive. "So what are you doing back here?"

"Edwin weren't the best painter . . . I tried to hawk his stuff, but no matter how cheap I priced it no one was having any of it. In the end I hid 'em here and gave Edwin the money I made selling other paintings. He was so half-cut most of the time he didn't notice. Listen, mister, whatever he's done, it ain't nothing to do with me. Why don't you leave me alone, eh?"

Correlli threatened to slap the old man again, who adopted a cowering fetal position. The fire-eater turned to Jonathan, his eyes narrowing.

"So this is Rafferty's gallery? I guess that's why you're here. You should have listened to me in the Midnight, Jonathan. I warned you to stop meddling. Where's Carnegie now?"

Behind Correlli, the door was edging open. Jonathan tensed, expecting another henchman, maybe even the horrific creature from the Panopticon coming to finish him off. Instead, Harry Pierce slipped silently into the room. Looking directly at Jonathan, he pressed a finger to his lips. He wasn't acting like a henchman. If anything, it looked like he was here to help.

"Look, I'm sorry," Jonathan stammered desperately. "Let me go, and I promise I'll stop. I'll never even go back to Darkside again."

Harry was clasping something in his hands. He trod carefully toward the fire-eater, his shoes making no sound on the floor.

Correlli shook his head. "It's not as simple as that, I'm afraid. You're getting too close. Who did you think you were dealing with? You've made one mistake too many. It's going to be your last."

As Correlli advanced threateningly, Jonathan took a pace back, but he was boxed in by all the crates, and there was nowhere to go. At the last second Harry Pierce stealthily covered the final few steps and brought the gargoyle sculpture from the other room down squarely on the back of Correlli's head.

21

The fire-eater toppled to the floor like a felled oak, and lay still. Harry dropped the sculpture, thew away the pistol, and winked at Jonathan.

"Pleased to see me?"

He was no longer wearing the black costume he had sported in the Cain Club and the Panopticon, but was dressed in the usual Darkside fashion. His old-fashioned waistcoat and cloth cap struck a strange note in the upscale London gallery.

"What are you *doing* here?" asked Jonathan.

"I've been tracking you since you first came into *The Informer* office. When you hurried off this morning, I knew it had to be important, so I tagged along behind you."

"You crossed over through the Heath?"

"Yes. I've never been to Lightside before. This place is crazy! All these cars racing around, not a horse in sight . . ."

"Forget about Lightside!" Jonathan cried angrily. "We thought you were the murderer! You've been following us around, and fighting us, and now you turn up and save my life! What do you think you're doing?"

The amusement faded from Harry's face. "Ah. Well, that's a longer story. I'll tell you when there's time."

Sol moaned with fear and tried to lift himself up. Harry jerked a thumb at him. "What's up with granddad?"

"He's a Darksider, too," replied Jonathan. "Though I think he wishes he weren't, right now."

The art dealer raised a hand to his forehead. "Please get out of here," he said weakly. "Take what you want, but please just go."

"I don't want to take anything," Jonathan said firmly. "I just want to look at the Spines. Then we'll go."

He moved over to the half-opened crate and peered through the gap. Inside there were four or five paintings, separated by thick layers of plastic packaging. One of them had to hold the key to this mystery. He felt his pulse rate quicken.

"This is all 'cause of Edwin?" Sol called over. "What's he done?"

"That's what I'm hoping to find out. He was murdered last week," Jonathan replied, trying in vain to lift up the lid. "This thing won't budge. Give us a hand, will you, Harry?"

The two boys were wrestling with the lid when a stirring noise alerted them to trouble. Correlli had clambered to his feet and was backing away from them, his eyes unsteady. Leaning back against a crate for support, he pointed a shaky finger at Jonathan and Harry.

"You're going to regret this. Children playing a man's game. You'll get your fingers burnt," he said. He pulled a brand from his belt and lit it with the smooth movement he had practiced so often that he could do it in his sleep, in the depths of the Midnight — or after a ringing blow to the head.

"NO!" Jonathan screamed, but it was too late. Correlli brought the brand to his lips, and rained fire down on the gallery.

Immediately the crates around them began to char and smoke like tinder. The fire-eater smiled with pleasure. Squealing, Sol ran for the exit. Harry charged at Correlli and hurled himself at the heavyset man, hitting him squarely in the chest with his shoulder. Still groggy, Correlli flew backward into a stack of crates, the brand flying from his hand and sparking off another fire across the other side of the room.

"Come on!" Harry shouted at Jonathan, waving his arm. "We've got to get out of here!"

In a daze, Jonathan obeyed the older boy, and they ran past the fire-eater and out into the safety of the gallery. It was only when they were halfway through the sculpture room that Jonathan's mind cleared and he stopped in his tracks.

"We have to go back!"

"Are you nuts?" cried Harry. "This place is going to burn to the ground!"

"We have to get Edwin's paintings! It's the only way we'll know what my mom found out!"

Harry pointed at the smoke seeping out underneath the storeroom door. "You'll get yourself killed!"

But it was too late. Jonathan was gone.

Flames were already raging at the far end of the storeroom, and the heat hit him like a brick wall. Correlli was nowhere to be seen. Ducking down to avoid the worst of the smoke, Jonathan put a handkerchief over his mouth and headed over to the Spine crate. To his dismay, he saw that most of the paintings were already on fire. Only the one nearest to him, sandwiched between two layers of smoldering packaging, looked retrievable. Wrapping his sleeves over his hands, Jonathan reached inside and carefully lifted it out. The rest of the paintings were burning even more fiercely: He was going to have to hope this was the right one. He clasped it underneath his arm and turned to leave the storeroom.

A hand snaked across the floor, grabbing Jonathan's ankle. Correlli was sprawled on his belly between two stacks of crates like a waiting predator, his snarling face looming up through the smoke. Yelling with surprise, Jonathan instinctively swung the painting and smacked the fire-eater in the face with the edge of the frame. Correlli grunted, but refused to let go. Jonathan could feel the smoke building up in his lungs; it was getting harder to breathe. He tried to jerk his leg free, but the fire-eater was incredibly strong.

"Let go!" Jonathan shouted, coughing. "Let go or we're both going to die!"

Correlli said nothing, only tightened his grip on

Jonathan's ankle. The boy looked around for something he could use as a weapon. He reached over to the closest stack of crates and tried to push the top one. It was incredibly heavy, and the task was only made more difficult by the disorienting effect of the heat and the smoke. One thing was clear, though: If he didn't move it, he was dead. His muscles straining, Jonathan redoubled his efforts and was rewarded with the sight of the crate shifting slowly toward the edge of the stack. Then, with a crash, it fell on top of Correlli, who bellowed with pain. The fire-eater released his grip, and Jonathan was free.

He stumbled toward the exit, tears streaming down his face. His skin felt like it was going to melt. Then he exploded through the door and back into the gallery, where he broke into a violent coughing fit. Harry swore, and dragged him out of the shop and into the fresh air beyond.

On the sidewalk outside, Jonathan bent double, trying to reclaim his breath. Passersby shot the pair startled looks. For now, the blaze was contained within the depths of the gallery, but it wouldn't be long before the elegant gold lettering on the shopfront would be melting into twisted, meaningless shapes.

"Sit down for a minute," Harry urged.

Jonathan shook his head. "No time. We have to get out of here. The fire department will be here soon."

Harry nodded back at the gallery "What about the other guy? He still in there?"

"Guess so. I don't want to be here if he gets out. Come on."

Still coughing, he led Harry quickly down the street, as the sound of wailing sirens started up far away.

If Alain Starling was surprised to see his son appear at the door with a blackened face and a strangely dressed companion by his side, he hid it well.

"Hello. I had a feeling I'd be seeing you again before too long. Are you OK?"

Jonathan nodded. "Yeah, I'm all right. At least you don't have to worry about me taking up smoking. Can we come in?"

They inspected the painting in the safety of the kitchen. Given that he had risked his life to retrieve it, Jonathan was entitled to feel a little disappointed with his prize. Suffering from years of neglect, the painting was caked with grime, which obscured whatever had been originally daubed on the canvas.

Alain wet his thumb and softly rubbed at one corner. "I think this'll come off," he said. "You go upstairs and tidy yourself up and I'll give this a cleaning in the meantime."

"Don't worry about that. I'll give you a hand."

Alain gave him a stern look. "No, you won't. You'll do what I say. Go on. Hop to it."

This hardly seemed like the time to stop for a wash, but there wasn't anything else he could do. Reluctantly, Jonathan trudged upstairs, feeling younger than he had in years. When he returned, cleaner, and in a fresh change of clothes, Alain and Harry were sitting in the living room. The painting had been propped up on the table, and a cloth had been draped over it.

"You took your time," Harry complained. "Your dad wouldn't let us look at it until you were here."

"Ready for the grand unveiling?" Alain said.

"Hang on a minute. Before we look at anything," Jonathan said, turning to Harry, "I want to know why we should trust you. I want to know why you're here, and why you've been following me."

Harry ran a hand through his hair. "I suppose that's fair enough. Look, I'm not trying to find out who killed Edwin or Nicholas or any of these guys from the Cain Club. And

I'm not trying to find out what happened to your mom, either."

"So what *are* you after?"

"I want to know who killed James Ripper," Harry said fiercely. "I'm going to find out who it was, and then I'm going to kill them."

The stark words echoed uncomfortably around the homely surroundings.

"I don't understand," Jonathan confessed. "He was killed years ago. Why should it matter to you?"

"Because he was my father. He was my father and someone killed him and I will avenge his death."

Jonathan stood there, stunned by the bald statement. Harry was a Ripper. He had thought the reporter to be nothing more than a preening idiot. But now, with the arrogant façade stripped away, he saw Harry in a new light. He saw an angry, hurt youth bent on revenge, who was more dangerous than any one of them could have guessed. And yet, at this moment, he was an ally.

As silence descended on the room, Harry stared at Jonathan. There were tears in his eyes.

"Is that a good enough reason for you?" he said bitterly.

"Yeah," Jonathan replied, thinking about his mom. "Yeah, that's good enough for me. So, do you want to see what this painting's about?"

Harry brushed the tears from his eyes and nodded.

They crowded around the table. Jonathan took hold of the cloth and pulled it away.

There was a pause, and then:

"I know this man," Alain said, blinking with surprise.

"Yes. I thought it was him," said Harry.

Jonathan just stared, speechless.

The frame was blackened and the corners of the painting singed, but it was still possible to make out the portrait of a young man, sitting idly in a large armchair. A mask was resting on top of his forehead, and his exposed face carried an expression of thoughtful uncertainty. A brass plate on the bottom of the frame named the painting as *Brother Fleet Comes to a Decision (DY106)*. It was the portrait of a Ripper and a murderer.

It was also, clearly and unmistakably, a portrait of the editor of *The Darkside Informer*, Lucien Fox.

22

The manicured calmness of Savage Row was a source of great pride for its inhabitants. The quiet informed passersby that the inhabitants here had acquired enough wealth to avoid the burly comings and goings of the Grand, and the everyday scuffling other Darksiders had to endure to make ends meet. Even the storm that was currently ravaging the rest of the borough appeared to be giving Savage Row a respectfully wide berth. Only the rustling of the leaves and the faint shimmering of the streetlamps gave evidence of any sort of life at all.

Until intruders from a much cheaper part of town had the temerity to disturb the silence, that is. Two sets of footsteps echoed underneath the trees: one long and measured, one heavy and labored. As they progressed down the avenue, Vendetta Heights rose in front of them like a black dragon. As if by some unspoken agreement, the two men came to a halt by a streetlamp, and Savage Row was silent once more.

Arthur Blake licked his lips nervously. "Are you sure this is a good idea?" he murmured.

Beside him, Carnegie snorted. "This is a dreadful idea. But you saw Raquella's note, didn't you? If William really is hiding out here, then we haven't got any choice. Anyway, I don't see what you've got to be nervous about. You didn't help the boy and his father nearly kill Vendetta."

"Nooooo . . ." replied Arthur slowly. "But I *did* write an article about the way his household staff tends to disappear, and suggested there was something fishy going on. By all accounts, he wasn't very pleased. Ever since then I've made staying out of his way a priority."

"You journalists are all the same. I see that your heroic editor's staying out of harm's way in the carriage back there." Carnegie jerked a thumb back up the road. "Hope he's warm enough."

Arthur sighed. "Don't be too hard on Lucien. He's barely well enough to leave the office, let alone creep around a mansion dodging homicidal maniacs."

"Call me an optimist, but I'm hoping that bit's not going to be too difficult. Vendetta's still recovering, and I doubt he'll be roaming around. Now, come on. We're standing out like sore thumbs here."

Though he was trying to sound confident, Carnegie was on edge. The encounter in the Panopticon had deeply unsettled him. In his mind, he kept replaying the moment the beast had come hurtling down from the watchtower toward him, shrouded in a dark cloud. And now, to make matters worse, he was back at Vendetta Heights. Having helped Jonathan defeat the vampire, Carnegie knew that one day he would be brought to account. He hadn't thought that he would be waltzing back through his front gates only a couple of months later. Not for the first time, Carnegie cursed the fact that he had ever met Jonathan.

As they neared the ivy-strewn stone gates, Arthur dipped into his black burglary bag and pulled out the grappling hook. He was about to start swinging when Carnegie caught his arm.

"I don't think that'll be necessary."

The wereman pushed against the left-hand gate, which swung open smoothly. He grinned wolfishly at the reporter.

"I know how fond you are of climbing, but seeing as the girl's unlocked the gates for us . . ."

"Are we going to knock on the front door, too?" asked Arthur, his voice dripping with sarcasm.

"Of course not. We're going around to the servants' entrance. Now hush!"

"This is madness," muttered the reporter, but under his breath.

Careful to avoid crunching up the gravel driveway, the two men padded across the lawn. In front of the mansion, the fountain was bathed in orange light, making the ornate sculpture of a crying child visible in the darkness. A solitary light burned in a window in the tower atop the east wing, like the eye of an evil beast. Aware that on his previous visit here he had been attacked by a swarm of vampire bats, Carnegie anxiously scanned the night sky for activity, but everything was still.

They looped around to the side of the mansion, careful to stay under the trees near the boundaries of the estate. The servants' entrance was well out of view from the driveway, down a flight of steps that led into the kitchen. To reach it, they were going to have to break from the cover of the trees. Refusing to hunch over or run, Carnegie walked boldly across the lawn and straight up to the building, where he descended the steps and found himself in a long, dark room. Arthur followed hot upon his heels, with a look on his face that suggested he'd rather be playing plummet in the Casino Sanguino than walking through this particular kitchen.

"Mr. Carnegie?"

Both men started as Raquella swished out of the gloom like a ghost.

"I'm sorry to startle you."

"That's all right, my dear. We're a bit twitchy tonight."

"I'm not surprised. The atmosphere in this place tends to put people on edge. My father is waiting for you. Follow me."

"Where's Vendetta?"

"In bed; asleep, I hope. I don't expect to see him until tomorrow afternoon."

"I hope you're right," said Arthur fervently.

The maid led them out of the kitchen, and up a narrow flight of stairs that came out on the ground floor. As they progressed along a corridor, they passed a door that stood slightly ajar. Arthur peered inside, and then whimpered softly. Carnegie glanced over his shoulder, and caught sight of large dark stains across the walls before Raquella closed the door. The beast within him stirred at the familiar scent of blood.

"I wouldn't go wandering around, if I were you," Raquella said firmly. "I wouldn't want you to get lost, or see anything you're not supposed to."

Sensing her guests' unease, she quickly ushered them toward a staircase and headed up past the first, second, and third floors, and into the tower where they had seen the light burning. Here the stairs began to spiral and the maid's heels clicked on the wooden steps. Carnegie could hear Arthur panting as the paunchy reporter struggled to keep up.

Thankfully, it wasn't long before they spotted light spilling out from underneath a door. Raquella went through it, and gestured for everyone else to follow. A pleasant contrast to the cold confines of the staircase, the room was warm, bright, and simply but elegantly furnished. A small fire crackled merrily in the hearth. And there, in a high-backed chair, idly flicking through a book, was Vendetta.

Raquella gasped.

"Master . . . what are you doing up? I thought you were asleep."

The vampire gave her an amused, calculating stare. "So I see." He closed his book with a snap. "I don't mind you inviting friends around, Raquella, but your taste leaves a little to be desired. What do we have here?" Vendetta cast an eye over his maid's companions. "A fat man and a pet mongrel. What a combination! Will they be dining with us?"

"It is late to be eating, sir, but if you are hungry I could . . ."

"I am always hungry, Raquella," he interrupted. "You of all people should know that."

Carnegie stepped in front of the maid. "Leave the girl alone. I forced her to let us in. Not her fault."

The vampire let out a scornful laugh. "Of course you did! It wasn't as if she wrote you a letter telling you her father was here, and you came racing straight over."

Carnegie glanced at Raquella, who blanched.

"I don't know how he knows," she protested. "I didn't tell him anything!"

"You didn't need to. Your disloyalty is so predictable.

Why do you think I told you about your father in the first place? I knew that you'd run off to Carnegie. I'm only surprised the Starling child isn't here."

"Well, we're here," said the wereman gruffly. "What do you want? Where's William?"

"William is fine. He's in a safe place, under lock and key. With a knife to his throat, just in case you get the urge to become all hairy and throttle me."

"I'll do what I can. My self-control stretches only so far."

"As does mine," Vendetta replied, his voice as low and cold as a grave. "If you touch me, the girl's father will have his throat slit. Continue to annoy me, and I might have him killed anyway."

"I'll ask again: What do you want?"

The wereman and the vampire stared at each other unflinchingly. Then Vendetta relaxed back into his chair with a smile.

"I was chatting to an old friend of mine from the Cain Club," he said, inspecting his nails, "and he told me you'd been blundering around there, causing trouble. And now the Gentlemen are being extinguished one by one. Except for our mutual friend Brother Steel, who's been enjoying my hospitality. All in all, I have the distinct impression you're in over your head again, Carnegie."

"It's you, isn't it?" Arthur's voice rang with shock. "You're Brother Fleet!"

The vampire shot the reporter a look of utter disdain.

"'Brother Fleet'?" he said contemptuously. "Secret societies . . . symbols and special handshakes . . . nothing more than schoolboy games. I have more pressing concerns. No, I am not Brother Fleet."

"That's a relief," Carnegie replied. "For a minute there I thought we were in trouble."

Vendetta chuckled. "In that, at least, we are in total agreement. By my logic, it's a matter of hours before you die very painfully. In a strange way, that's what stopped me from having you killed the minute you entered my house. Do you really think we're alone?"

Carnegie pushed his hat up and scratched his forehead. "It appears you have the advantage on us."

"It does, rather. I am looking forward to finding out exactly how much you're going to suffer: It might almost make my recent illness worthwhile."

"Yes. I heard that you hadn't been feeling well. I do hope life hasn't been *too* hard for you."

Vendetta bared his fangs and hissed at Carnegie. Arthur edged back toward the door.

"Enough!" spat the vampire. "I would deal with you myself, had I the strength. Get out of here, and take William with you: He is no longer welcome in the house. No matter where you go, it will not take long for Brother Fleet to catch up with you. I am glad you will spend your remaining few hours fleeing like rats."

"Where is William?"

Vendetta rang a small bell, and a door opened in the wall. A greasy-haired man frog-marched William into the room, one hand wrapped in his hair, the other holding a knife to his throat. Carnegie saw another flash of movement, and noted a third hand poking out from the henchman's waistcoat, holding a small pistol that was trained on the wereman.

"Father!" Raquella shouted.

"I'm all right, child," William said, with difficulty. "Stay calm."

"You can let him go now, Yann."

The smarmy man nodded, and stepped away from William. He kept the pistol firmly trained on Carnegie.

William Joubert hugged his daughter tightly, then nodded at Vendetta with a familiarity that surprised the wereman.

"Time to leave," he said briskly. "Raquella will come to no harm?"

"No promises," Vendetta replied. "I'll see what I can do."

William looked at his daughter tenderly. "Stay here. Believe it or not, this is the safest place for you right now."

And with that, he spun on his heel and headed down the stairs.

The three men hurried down the driveway of Vendetta Heights and out onto Savage Row. Even as they strode along the broad avenue Carnegie didn't feel any safer for having left the vampire's lair behind. He could smell violence in the air. It was only a matter of time now. The wereman could feel an invisible net tightening around them all.

Their carriage was waiting for them at the bottom of Savage Row. Lucien was sat up in the driver's seat, his skel-etal body muffled against the cold in a thick black overcoat with the collar turned up. As William and Arthur climbed into the carriage, Carnegie went around to speak to the editor.

"You know what you're doing up there?"

Lucien picked up the reins and nodded. "*The Informer's* got a safe house on Puck Avenue, the other side of town. We've used it in the past to interview sources and hide reporters. William should be safe there, for a few days at least."

"Sounds like a good plan. You'll have to go ahead without me, though. The boy should be back at my office by now. I have a feeling things are going to get very nasty very quickly, and I don't want him on his own."

"Why don't we just go via Fitzwilliam Street?"

Carnegie shook his head. "No time. William's the priority. I'll catch up with you as soon as I can. Don't stop for anything."

The editor nodded and tightened his cloak around himself. William called Carnegie over from the carriage window.

"I'm sorry you have been dragged into this. I never helped them, you know . . . killing James. They ostracized me because of it, did everything they could to make my life a misery afterward. It seems now I will have to pay the ultimate price."

Carnegie shook his head. "You'll be all right, William. I promise."

The wereman banged on the side of the carriage, and watched as it sailed off into the night.

The storm over the Grand had eased off by the time Carnegie arrived back at Fitzwilliam Street, but pools of brown water were still eddying in the gutters. The wereman splashed across the cobblestones and up the stairs to his lodgings. His night had been so full of surprises that he barely registered the fact that Jonathan was deep in conversation with Harry. At the sight of Carnegie, Jonathan leapt to his feet.

"Where's William?" he asked.

"He's fine. Lucien and Arthur are taking him to a safe house across town. I came here to pick you up and . . ."

"Oh no!" Jonathan cried, and his face crumpled.

"What is it now?"

It was Harry who responded.

"Lucien's Brother Fleet. He's the Ripper. You've just sent William to his death."

23

Elias Carnegie stood on the carriage like a charioteer, staring at the road ahead, the reins in his hands and death on his mind. The carriage tore through the streets of Darkside, like a comet, rocking dangerously from side to side over the cobblestones.

The wereman's snarls carried to inside the cab, where Harry shot Jonathan a questioning glance.

"He's on our side, right?"

Jonathan didn't say anything. He had seen Carnegie angry before, but never as driven as this. Back in the lodgings, the wereman had listened to Harry's story without saying a word, even when the young man had confessed the identity of his father. But as Harry went on, a muscle began to twitch in Carnegie's cheek.

"In the beginning I didn't know that Lucien had anything to do with James's death. I only joined *The Informer* because I thought it would provide cover for my own investigations. But then I broke into the Cain Club and saw him about to burn that newspaper article. It looked suspicious, so I jumped in to try and stop him . . ."

". . . only we turned up, and got it the wrong way around," Jonathan added.

"Yeah. And after that, I didn't know who to trust. I went to the Panopticon hoping to get some answers from de Quincy, but ended up running into that . . . *thing* up in the watchtower." Harry shivered. "I heard de Quincy screaming as I came in through the window. It was pitch-black, though, and I couldn't see anything. Then from nowhere this creature was on me. It was all I could do to throw myself out of the window. I'll tell you straight — I've seen some pretty horrible things in Darkside, and nothing's ever scared me before. But the creature in that room just made me want to run away and hide."

Jonathan thought back to his encounter in his Panopticon, and how even the sight of the cloud had chilled him to the bone. He was amazed that Harry had stood toe to toe with the creature and survived. Carnegie, on the other hand, looked distinctly unimpressed. He loomed over Harry.

"This is all fascinating stuff, but why don't we cut to the chase? Why don't you tell me where your uncle's taken William Joubert?"

"Hey!" cried Jonathan. "That's not fair!"

Harry's eyes flashed dangerously. "He's no uncle of mine, half-breed. I've no idea where he's gone, but I'll track him down, and I'll make him pay. You have my word on that."

"Is that so?" hissed the wereman. "You'll have to get in line, son." He glanced over at Jonathan. "Time to get moving."

"Where?"

It was Harry who answered. "The Cain Club. That's where it all started. That's where my father was most powerful. Lucien'll want his final victory to be there."

Carnegie began moving toward the door, then paused and looked meaningfully at the young Ripper.

"I gave William my word he'd be safe. We're going to find him tonight, if I have to tear Darkside down brick by brick. So if you even think about getting in my way, you're going to regret it."

Now they were racing across town against the merciless ticking of the clock, in the desperate hope that William and Arthur were still alive. A cold killer awaited them, a merciless Ripper.

The first streaks of dawn were smearing the early morning sky by the time Jonathan saw the Cain Club coming into view. Its patrons had long since beaten a merry retreat back to their mansions, and the windows were dark and lifeless. Even the doormen had abandoned their usual posts at the front entrance.

Tugging furiously on the reins, Carnegie brought the horses to a halt by the steps, and Jonathan and Harry hopped out of the cab. The wereman made a final check of his possessions, and Jonathan was shocked to see a gleaming array of weaponry strapped to his body. Carnegie looked up and saw him staring.

"Bad things are going to happen in here, boy. The pair of you would be better off staying in the carriage."

"No way," Jonathan replied fiercely. "We've come this far together. And this isn't just about William, remember? What about my mom?"

"And my dad," said Harry. "I'm in too."

The wereman shrugged. "Fine. It's your funeral."

And with that, he strode up to the doors. Sizing up the thick wood, he reached into his pockets and pulled out a bottle of his Special Recipe. After soaking the doors with a thick coating of the liquid, he retreated behind a pillar and gestured for the boys to do the same. Then he flicked a match into life on his grizzled cheek, and tossed it toward the entrance.

Even pressed up tightly against a pillar, Jonathan was nearly knocked off his feet by the force of the blast. Planks flew past his nose like giant matchsticks, and the air was filled with smoke and the smell of charred wood. His ears ringing with the sound of the explosion, Jonathan stepped gingerly out from behind the pillar and surveyed the damage. The doors had been blown from their hinges, and angry flames were licking the scarred frame. Through the smoke, he could see the plush interior of the Cain Club.

Carnegie stepped over the rubble and into the building. Jonathan glanced at Harry, and was strangely reassured to see the fear in his eyes. Both of them knew that there was a real chance they wouldn't leave the Cain Club alive. Jonathan picked up a couple smoldering planks of wood, and tossed one to Harry.

"I think you might need this."

Harry grimaced. "It'll have to do. After you."

And in that, for the first time, Jonathan heard a note of respect in his voice. The two of them stepped over the threshold.

The last time Jonathan had been in the Cain Club, he had been struck by the air of preening complacency and comfort. But now, with the hallways cleared of the braying members, and the gas lamps burning low on the walls, it had assumed an altogether more sinister atmosphere. On the grand staircase, the upper floors were shrouded in darkness. Each doorway was an unspoken threat. Carnegie hesitated as he weighed the different options, then strode purposefully up the stairs and onto the first floor.

It was impossible to know how long they spent wandering though the labyrinth of identical rooms and corridors. Time seemed to lose all meaning. To Jonathan, whose nerves were shredded by the silence, every second seemed like an hour. It was a struggle to keep control of himself: More than once, he swung his plank at an invisible assailant. His senses had gone into overdrive: He could hear Carnegie's rasping breaths, more beast now than man; could see Harry losing himself in thoughts of murderous revenge; and could almost taste his own fear.

And then there were figures up ahead, lounging lazily against the corridor walls. Four men, their faces covered in the grotesque masks that marked them out as members of the club. Jagged rips ran down their suit jackets, and their white shirts were splattered with blood. All of them were carrying knives. At the sight of the intruders, one of them swaggered to the front of the group.

"What have we here?" he sneered to his companions. "They don't look like members. They don't dress like members. You know, I've got a feeling they shouldn't be here at all."

"In that case," replied another, "we're going to have to hurt them. This is a private club, after all."

Carnegie growled. "This is not your fight. Go away now and I'll let you live."

The leader giggled. "How kind of you!" He brandished his knife. "Now come here, mutt, and let me house-train you."

They rushed as one, weapons raised aloft. Two men engaged Carnegie, while the others split up and made for the boys. Jonathan heard Harry cry out in alarm, and was then forced to duck as a knife whistled over his head. Overbalanced, his assailant grunted as Jonathan swung the plank into his midriff. He followed up with an instinctive charge that sent the man crashing to the ground. Jonathan was about to make a grab for the knife when a heavy hand restrained him. He whirled around, plank raised, only to see Carnegie's matted face.

"I'll take it from here."

The bodies of the two men who had attacked the wereman were sprawled out on the floor. Carnegie wasn't even breathing heavily. Unusually for him, he had fought in silence. There was a glint of satisfaction in his eyes, and Jonathan knew that Carnegie felt better with his claws out and the beast rage coursing through his veins. Beyond him Harry was standing over another body, hands on his knees, shaken but unharmed.

The remaining attacker made a futile lunge at Carnegie, who almost absentmindedly kicked the knife from his hand and sent him sprawling across the carpet.

"Wait around the corner," he said. "This won't take long."

Normally Jonathan would have argued with him, but this time he thought better of it. Not tonight. Instead, he took Harry by the elbow and led him down the corridor. They waited for the sound of screaming, but it never came.

After a few seconds, Carnegie came walking calmly around the corner.

"He didn't wait for me to ask any questions. Took a poison pill instead."

"Looks like we're on the right track, though."

"Maybe. Stay close to me. You're not really built for this."

They had barely gone two steps when the quiet was brutally shattered by a cry for help. Jonathan didn't recognize the owner, but at once Carnegie was sprinting away. Jonathan raced after him, deeper into the building, taking the stairs two at a time and praying that the wereman's acute hearing was leading them in the right direction.

He had always prided himself on his speed, and had put it to the test many times over the years, but there was no way he could keep up with Carnegie. The wereman ate up the ground with his loping stride, his overcoat flapping behind him. Jonathan was struggling not to lose him. Luckily Harry was with them: A fit young man who was also consumed with rage, he overtook Jonathan and kept the wereman in sight. Just as Jonathan felt his lungs were going to burst like balloons, he crashed through a side door and found himself standing on a first-floor gallery.

Carnegie had come to a halt by the railings, while Harry had ducked down out of sight behind the balustrade. Both were looking out over a macabre scene.

The great dining hall of the Cain Club had been witness to some of the loudest and longest revelries in Darkside. Two hundred feet long, it housed two great oaken dining tables that ran the length of the hall. At the far end of the room, beneath a giant relief of the club's crest, stood a raised platform where Jonathan guessed the most esteemed members of the club were allowed to sit and lord over the rest of the diners. Unlike the rest of the Cain Club, there were no photographs or paintings on the walls, which had been painted a deep shade of red. Nor were there any windows, ensuring that no natural light could seep into the hall. Instead, a phalanx of flaming sconces had been placed along the two tables, providing a fiery guard of honor along the aisle.

William Joubert was standing on the platform. His arms had been bound to the entwined letter "C"s on the club crest, high above his head. Someone had torn the shirt from his back, and his torso was covered in red welts. His head was lolling to one side: It was clear he had been beaten. Arthur was lying slumped at his feet, unconscious.

And then there was the third man in the hall, sitting quietly on the edge of the platform, his hands clasped together. At the sound of the door crashing open, he rose awkwardly to his feet and addressed the balcony, his arms outstretched in welcome.

"Good evening, gentlemen," said Lucien. "I've been expecting you."

24

They had searched for him across Darkside, faced down threats in the Midnight and the Cain Club, encountered the very soul of terror in the Panopticon. In Lightside, Jonathan had nearly burned himself alive in order to discover his identity. And all that time, Brother Fleet had been sitting in the offices of *The Darkside Informer*.

Looking down at him now, Jonathan struggled to match the frail figure with the evil mastermind he had imagined. Lucien had drawn himself into a crooked stance that favored his good leg, but his gaze was direct and composed, and hardened in a way Jonathan hadn't seen before.

"Why don't you come down and join us?" Lucien called up to the balcony in his familiar baritone. "I'm sure Arthur and William would be glad of the company."

Carnegie licked his lips nervously, sizing up the situation. Apart from the three men down below, the hall looked empty, but the shadows promised all sorts of unpleasant surprises.

"Are they still alive?"

"Oh yes. For now." Lucien limped over to Arthur's prone body, and dragged his head up by his hair. "Though I wouldn't dawdle, if I were you. Who knows what I might do if I'm left alone with them?"

He looked up and grinned, and suddenly Jonathan was left in no doubt as to exactly who he was dealing with. He was Lucien Fox; he was Brother Fleet. He was a Ripper, and he had murdered his own flesh and blood.

"Wait!" Carnegie called out. "We're coming." As he spoke, the wereman retrieved something from his pocket and passed it surreptitiously down to Harry, who was still crouched down out of sight.

In one swift movement the wereman flipped himself over the balustrade and swooped down from the balcony, landing in an easy crouch on one of the great tables. He turned and looked up expectantly at Jonathan, waiting for him to follow suit. The drop down to the hall was severe, but Jonathan didn't want to draw any more attention to the balcony and Harry. Swinging his legs over the balustrade, he took a deep breath and dropped down. He landed on the table hard, his knees jarring at the impact. Lucien's eyes widened.

"Jonathan! I'm surprised to see you! I gave Correlli strict instructions not to let you live."

"He tried his best," Jonathan shot back, hoping he sounded more brave than he felt. "Heard from him recently?"

Lucien nodded as if in approval. "A spirited response. I see you take after your mother in that respect. She was full of brave words, too . . . at first."

Without thinking, Jonathan scrambled off the table and headed for Lucien, a combustible mixture of hate and adrenaline in his veins. Until a large paw clapped down on his shoulder, halting his progress.

"What did you do to my mom?" Jonathan roared, trying to break free. "If you hurt her, I'll kill you!"

"Not now, boy," Carnegie said, his claws digging into Jonathan's shoulder. "Not now."

Lucien broke into a mocking peal of laughter. "How very touching. Teaching self-restraint these days, Carnegie?"

"When I can," the wereman replied coolly. "You teaching running?"

The smile faded from the Ripper's face. He climbed down from the platform and hobbled painfully toward Carnegie.

"I expected better from you," he said in a deathly whisper. "I've heard all those jokes before. My friends at the Cain Club called me Brother Fleet, remember?" Lucien gestured at his twisted leg. "They thought that was funny. Of course, I would never go anywhere quickly like this. They treated me as a joke, and I was a *Ripper*. I could have killed them anytime I wanted. But instead I bit my tongue and bided my time, waiting until they could be of use to me.

"When I discovered my dear brother's identity, I knew I could appeal to their vanity and get them to help me. Without their aid, I could never get close enough to the esteemed James Arkel to lure him into a trap. And, predictably, one by one they fell in line. All except for Brother Steel." He turned back to the captive William. "How does it feel to be back in the Cain Club? Have the last few years been enjoyable for you, my friend? I've had such fun blocking your pathetic attempts to carve a life for yourself. It's proved much more satisfying than killing you would ever have been."

William raised his head weakly, and spat a glob of blood onto the platform floor.

"I've been happy," he croaked. "I've had my wife, my children . . . but then I wouldn't expect you to understand that."

"Well, my family works slightly differently from everyone else's, as Nicholas and the rest of the Gentlemen knew. They tried to take advantage of that fact. They still thought I was weak. As you've seen, they were wrong. I taught them the same lesson I taught James."

"You?" Carnegie spat mockingly. "You don't do anything, cripple. You stand back and watch as your creature does your dirty work for you."

Lucien shot him a look of pure hatred.

"Keep your foul mouth shut. What would you know about the dealings of the Rippers?"

"Enough to know that James would have beaten you to a pulp if you had faced him like a man. I'm amazed you had the guts to attack him while he was awake."

"Face him like a man?" The Ripper broke into a peal of laughter. "And why on Darkside would I need to do that?

I have a Black Phoenix, a creature born of evil and shrouded in the night. What need have I of a man?"

And then the horrifying shriek from the Panopticon was assaulting their ears again. Carnegie whirled around.

"Where's it coming from?" he shouted above the din.

Jonathan tugged on the wereman's coat, the blood draining from his face. A low moan escaped from his lips.

The shrieking sound was coming from Lucien's throat.

"My God," breathed Carnegie.

Lucien's head was flung back, and his eyes bunched tightly shut. As they watched, he spread his arms out in an ecstatic gesture, and his body began to twitch and writhe, like a puppet whose strings had been shaken. Waves churned across the Ripper's chest, and with horror Jonathan saw his ribs straining to break through his flesh. Lucien screamed with pain — an unexpectedly human sound — and fell to his knees. His skin darkened and bubbled as it changed form. Then the man was gone, and there was a creature where he had been.

At first glance, the Black Phoenix might have been mistaken for a majestic bird: a huge, sleek creature cloaked in jet-black feathers. But a closer look revealed it to be an abomination. Its feathers were lank and greasy, and reeked of rotting meat. Its wings were leathery, and crisscrossed by sickly red veins. Its beak and talons were the color of curdled milk, and stained with blood.

The Phoenix raised its head and inspected them, two beady eyes gleaming with malice.

Carnegie didn't wait. He pulled out two pistols and started firing. The hall was filled with the sound of gunshots and the smell of cordite. The Black Phoenix screeched with anger and wrapped its thick wings around itself. Carnegie didn't stop until he had unloaded the chambers of both weapons. As the last echo died away, Jonathan saw the bullets strewn at the Phoenix's feet. The creature unfurled its wings, and cawed with pleasure.

Carnegie turned to Jonathan. "Worth a try," he said defensively.

"What are we going to do now?"

The wereman shrugged. "What can we do? You got anything stronger than bullets? I told you not to come with me, boy. You really are an irritating little flea, you know that?"

Jonathan realized too late that that was Carnegie's way of saying good-bye. Before he could stop him, the wereman roared and charged across the hall. The creature lifted itself off the ground and prepared to meet him, the first tendrils of black cloud rolling out from beneath its flapping wings. Jonathan's blood ran cold.

Having failed to wound the Phoenix using pistols, Carnegie attacked it in the way he knew best: at close quarters, with fists and claws flying. He moved with fearsome speed and power, but even as he disappeared into the thickening fog Jonathan knew that he was doomed. Carnegie was a being of flesh and blood, and the Black Phoenix a thing of pure evil. As the wereman's agonized shouts drowned out the sounds of combat, Jonathan desperately wanted to rush in and help his friend, but his muscles had locked with fear.

A lung-bursting yell from the balcony broke the spell. Jonathan looked up to see Harry Pierce throwing himself from the balcony, reaching up for one of the great chandeliers suspended from the ceiling. It looked like a suicidal leap, but somehow Harry kept rising through the air like a rocket, until his hand fastened onto the chandelier. There was a shriek of annoyance from within the cloud, and suddenly the Phoenix began arrowing toward the boy. Harry waited until the creature was almost upon him before hurling a bottle into the shifting black cloud with his free hand and then letting go of the chandelier. He fell like a stone, hitting the floor with a loud crunch.

Where the cloud had lifted, Jonathan was able to see the prone form of Carnegie. The wereman's body was crumpled, and lying in a pool of blood. Limply, the detective summoned the strength to raise a hand, and pointed at one of the torches. Of course! Carnegie had given Harry a bottle of something before getting off the balcony — his Special Recipe!

Up by the chandelier, the black cloud had temporarily paused with surprise. Stung into action, Jonathan grabbed the nearest torch and raced across the hall. He stood over Harry's body, brandishing the flame. Through the shifting waves of the cloud, he caught a glimpse of the Phoenix shrieking with anticipation, its neck muscles twisting and its beak snapping. Then it was hurtling toward him. Jonathan threw the torch as hard as he could, and dived on top of Harry.

There was a huge roaring sound, like a waterfall, and the creature was coated in a sheet of flames. It flapped its wings frantically, sending wave after wave of darkness out into the hall. But the flames still kept burning, and the

Phoenix's screeches were becoming more desperate. Jonathan pressed his hands over his ears as it fell to the floor with a thunderous crash, and lay still.

Then, silence. Light began to tiptoe back into the hall, revealing bodies scattered across the floor: Carnegie bleeding, Harry motionless, the hulking form of the Black Phoenix, smoke plumes rising from its feathers. Jonathan picked himself up and walked slowly over to the creature. He heard a soft cawing, more like a crooning than anything else, and realized that the Black Phoenix was still clinging on to life.

The bird lifted its head groggily as it sensed the boy approaching. And then, with its left eye, winked at Jonathan.

He barely had time to gasp before the bird brought back one of its huge wings and swatted him. Jonathan went flying across the floor, crashing into the side of one of the great tables. He lay there, groaning. There was a sharp pain in his chest, and he wondered if he had broken a rib. It felt like he had been hit by a car.

His heart sinking, Jonathan realized they had made a foolish error. Of course the Special Recipe hadn't hurt the creature. Phoenixes were fire-loving. After the initial shock of the impact, the bird had simply lapped up the flames.

He heard the sound of talons clicking on the wooden floor of the hall, and the smell of rotting meat grew stronger than ever. The Black Phoenix pressed a sharp talon down on Jonathan's chest. He cried out with pain. Ever so gently, the bird began to increase the pressure on the boy's lungs. Jonathan closed his eyes, and hoped that the end would be swift.

"I think that's enough," said a familiar voice from the back of the hall.

25

Marianne leaned lazily against the door frame, her face creased with arch amusement. Her hair was dyed a startling shade of neon green and tied back in a ponytail. She was dressed in a full undertaker's suit, right down to the long black ribbons hanging down from her top hat. A large crossbow was cradled easily in her arms. Behind her, Humble and Skeet stood in solemn attendance.

"Leave the boy alone."

The Phoenix cocked its head with surprise, and let out one of its unholy screeches. Marianne stepped away from the doorway and raised her crossbow.

"I mean it, Lucien. Get away from the boy and change back into your normal form."

Jonathan felt the pressure ease on his chest, and lifted

his head to see the Phoenix advance threateningly on the bounty hunter. Marianne smiled faintly.

"I think Lucien wants to play, boys. Shall we oblige?"

The mute nodded and raised a heavy ax in the air. Jabbering and bounding on the spot, Skeet drew a sword. With practiced ease, the three slipped into fighting formation.

"You may have bested Carnegie and a couple of children," Marianne called out. "But you'll find that Humble, Skeet, and I are a slightly tougher proposition. I wonder just how long you can maintain that form for . . ."

Even as she spoke, there was a shimmering where the Black Phoenix was standing. To the sound of tearing and cracking, it began to fold in on itself, writhing wings shrinking back into the damaged shell that was Lucien Fox's body. The shrieks died away, to be replaced by human cries of pain. Then there was only the shape of a small, thin man sprawled on the floor, coughing.

Marianne cast a critical eye over his disheveled form.

"So — you would be my brother. I have to say, I'd rather hoped for more."

On the other side of the room, the final jigsaw pieces fit together in Jonathan's mind. Marianne was a Ripper. She had been the recipient of the other blackmail letter from Nicholas. That was why she had shown such an interest in their investigation! They had done her dirty work for her, and led her straight to the very man she wanted.

Lucien glared up at her.

"It's you?" he spat. "What are you doing here?"

Marianne smiled sweetly.

"I wanted to see what the inside of the Cain Club looked like. The members get so nervous about the thought of a lady passing through the doors." She looked around, and wrinkled her nose. "Although now that I'm here, I'm not sure it was worth it. It's a bit gothic for my tastes."

Jonathan started as a bloodied hand touched his shoulder. He looked around to see Carnegie's face, a mass of purple bruises and matted hair. One of the wereman's eyes was swollen shut, and he was clutching his right arm.

"Carnegie!"

"S'all right, boy," he slurred. "Had worse. Come on."

Slipping an arm over the wereman's shoulder, Jonathan pulled himself to his feet, biting back a cry of pain. Harry lay immobile on the floor nearby, his rib cage shifting slightly with each shallow breath. The boy and the wereman made their way slowly over to the entrance of the hall, where Lucien had been forced into an upright position. He winced as Skeet prodded him with his sword.

Marianne grinned as she saw Jonathan and Carnegie near. "Hello there. Lovely day, isn't it?"

A low rumbling noise emanated from the wereman's throat. "Stop playing around, Marianne."

The bounty hunter gave him a cold, appraising stare.

"I'll do exactly what I want. If you'd rather, I could leave and you could continue your disagreement with my brother. The way you two look right now, I'm not entirely sure who would win."

She turned to Lucien, her icy composure the polar opposite of his furious seething.

"On second thought, little brother, get out of my sight. You disgust me. I know you now, and will be watching out for you. Our father's time is short, and we *will* meet afterward."

"I look forward to it," Lucien replied. "I wonder if you'll beg for mercy like James did."

Marianne flinched, and her brother laughed. He was hobbling out of the hall when a thick, hairy arm blocked his progress.

"I hate to interrupt this game of happy families," said Carnegie gruffly, "but could someone explain to me why I'm going to let this man walk free? You might be squeamish about polishing him off, Marianne, but I'd positively relish it."

The bounty hunter shook her head. "This is between myself and my brother — it is no business of yours, wereman. If you try to intervene, I'll stop you."

"But, Marianne," Jonathan protested, "Lucien's pure evil. If you let him go now, he'll try to kill you!"

"I know *exactly* what he'll do. That's how I'll be able to stop him." Marianne gave Lucien one final glance. "Your day of reckoning will come. But it won't be here, or in some dingy backstreet. It will be at the Blood Succession, as it was for all the Rippers that came before us. Then you'll pay for James's murder with your life."

"We'll see, sister," Lucien replied. With one final venomous glance, he hobbled slowly out of the hall.

As Carnegie clambered up to the platform to untie William, Marianne attached the crossbow to her belt and fixed Jonathan with a brilliant smile.

"It seems you've lived to fight another day, little one."

"Just about. Are you disappointed?" he challenged.

She chuckled with delight. "Maybe a little. Still, I *did* save your life."

"Yeah . . ." Jonathan paused, unsure of what to say. "Um . . . thanks, I guess."

"You're welcome. And get those ribs strapped up as soon as you can."

The bounty hunter turned to leave.

"Oh, Marianne? Could you do me a favor?"

"A favor? Perhaps."

"I've just survived a fight with a Black Phoenix. Do you think you could stop calling me 'little one'?"

She smiled enigmatically and, with a flick of her undertaker's coat, was gone.

It was a battered and bruised party that stumbled back through the corridors of the Cain Club, their faces streaked with ash and blood. Jonathan walked slightly bent over, holding his ribs. Arthur walked alongside him, bleary-eyed, but unhurt save for a sizable bump on his forehead. Behind them Carnegie leaned on Harry as he limped along, his right arm dangling by his side. It was William Joubert who led the way, his clothes torn and his body covered in cuts and bruises, but striding with dignity out through the main hall and into the early-morning sunshine.

After the horror they had witnessed indoors, it was a blessed relief to stumble out onto the steps and inhale the dubious delights of the Darkside air. The carriage was waiting for them where Carnegie had abandoned it. Arthur hauled himself up into the driver's seat.

"Well, as fun as this has been, gentlemen, I have to go back to *The Informer*. I've got an article to write." Arthur's eyes twinkled. "I think it might just make the front page."

"Need a hand?" Harry called out.

"You?!"

"Well, you've lost an editor, and I'm rather free for now. I was kind of enjoying the whole journalism thing."

Arthur sighed. "Get in. Anyone else?"

"You can take me," William replied. "I need to see my family." He clasped Carnegie's hand. "Thank you, Elias," he said simply.

The wereman wiped his nose on his sleeve, and looked away. "Gave you my word, didn't I?"

Harry helped William into the carriage, and followed him inside. He pulled down the window and smiled at Jonathan.

"We did all right in the end, didn't we?"

"Not bad for a couple of kids."

"You not coming with us?"

Jonathan glanced at Carnegie. "I think we'll walk."

Arthur gee'd up the horses, and the carriage moved away down the street. And then it was just the pair of them again, standing on the steps. The wereman noticed the downcast expression on Jonathan's face.

"What's up, boy?"

Jonathan looked down at his feet. "Look, I know we survived and everything . . . but Lucien's gone and I didn't find out anything more about my mom. I've never going to learn what happened, am I?"

Carnegie barked with amusement, then winced with the pain the laughter caused him.

"You're something else, boy. We luck out of a certain death situation, and you're complaining that you didn't get enough answers. What were you going to do — ask the Black Phoenix a few searching questions?"

Jonathan chuckled humorlessly, and shrugged.

"Listen to me," the wereman continued matter-of-factly. "Not only are we going to have to deal with Vendetta when he's recovered, but now we've crossed a Ripper as well. To be honest, I think our chances of surviving to the end of the week are fairly slim. You're not going to be short on contact with bad guys. I'm sure you'll get the opportunity to ask them a question or two."

"That's true," came the glum reply. "But if things are so dangerous, why do you sound so cheery?"

Carnegie shrugged. "Must be my sunny disposition. Come on."

He turned and limped down the steps of the Cain Club. Jonathan trotted after him.

"Hey, wait! Where are we going? I need to bandage my ribs!"

"No time. We have an appointment with a certain lady with a special ring, remember?"

Jonathan scratched his head. Then it came to him suddenly, though it felt like an age ago.

"Felicity Haverwell? After all we've been through, you want to go chasing after *her*?"

Carnegie tugged the lapels on his suit jacket, and pushed the stovepipe hat back on his forehead.

"Matter of pride, boy. After all, I have got a business to think of. Can't let word get around that I'm going soft."

"I somehow doubt that's going to happen," Jonathan replied, and the pair of them headed out into the grimy Darkside morning.